"It was a crush, I thought—"

"Maybe a bit more than that." Chance shook his head. "You two fell in love, and I sorted out my feelings privately. That's how I do things, if you hadn't noticed."

And she'd spent years cozying up to her future brother-in-law, never realizing how difficult she was probably making it for him.

They were silent for a few seconds, and Sadie's heart welled with regret. He met her gaze once more, and she saw a flicker of a smile on his face.

"And now?" she asked hesitantly.

"Sadie, that's all in the past," he said. "Just a little nostalgia. It's under control." Those blue eyes met hers once more, then he heaved a long sigh. "Trust me on that."

"Okay." She nodded.

"So back to business."

She had questions, but she wasn't even sure what they were right now, or if she should ask them. She sucked in a wavering breath and looked at her notes.

"Yes, back to business."

Patricia Johns writes from Alberta, Canada. She has her Hon. BA in English literature and currently writes for Harlequin's Love Inspired, Western Romance and Heartwarming lines. You can find her at patriciajohnsromance.com.

Books by Patricia Johns

Love Inspired

Comfort Creek Lawmen

Deputy Daddy
The Lawman's Runaway Bride

His Unexpected Family
The Rancher's City Girl
A Firefighter's Promise
The Lawman's Surprise Family

Harlequin Western Romance

The Cowboy's Christmas Bride
The Cowboy's Valentine Bride
The Triplets' Cowboy Daddy
Her Cowboy Boss

Harlequin Heartwarming

A Baxter's Redemption
The Runaway Bride
A Boy's Christmas Wish

Visit the Author Profile page at Harlequin.com for more titles.

The Lawman's Runaway Bride

Patricia Johns

HARLEQUIN® LOVE INSPIRED®

Recycling programs
for this product may
not exist in your area.

LOVE INSPIRED BOOKS

ISBN-13: 978-1-335-42790-8

The Lawman's Runaway Bride

Copyright © 2018 by Patty Froese Ntihemuka

www.Harlequin.com

Printed in U.S.A.

Every wise woman buildeth her house:
but the foolish plucketh it down with her hands.
—*Proverbs* 14:1

To my husband and our son.
Life is so much sweeter together!

Chapter One

Chance Morgan tucked his chief-of-police hat under his arm as he jogged up the worn wooden staircase to the second floor of Comfort Creek's town hall. He rubbed a hand over his short-cropped sandy-blond hair. There were times he thought it was working with the mayor that had caused the premature gray at his temples. He was five minutes early for his meeting with Mayor Scott, and he was dreading it already.

Mayor Eugene Scott was planning a remembrance ceremony for the four men from Comfort Creek, Colorado, killed in the military over the last five years. The mayor's son was one of them, as was Chance's fraternal twin brother, and since both Chance and Mayor Scott had someone close to them die overseas, the mayor figured they wanted the same thing.

He was wrong, of course. Chance was a private man, and while he grieved his brother deeply, he didn't like having to do that in front of the entire town. Regardless, when the mayor summoned, the chief of police showed up—he glanced at his watch—four minutes early.

"Good morning, Chief." Brenda, the middle-aged secretary, shot him a smile from her desk. Her hair was tucked behind her ears, along with a pen, and she was clicking through something on her computer screen that seemed to be absorbing most of her attention.

"Is he in?" Chance asked.

"Go on through," Brenda said, turning back to her computer. "He's waiting for you."

Chance settled what he hoped was an appropriately professional look on his face, and tapped on the closed office door, then opened it. He could see Mayor Scott behind a mammoth mahogany desk. His bald head had a thin strip of hair swept over the top of it, and his dress shirt was already open at the neck despite the snow on the ground outside.

"Chief Morgan," the mayor said. "Come on in."

Chance opened the door the rest of the way, and as he did, it revealed a slim woman sitting in the visitor's chair. His heart stopped for second, and then did three fast beats to catch up. Sadie Jenkins…

"Hi, Chance."

She wore a pair of gray dress pants paired with a pink cashmere sweater that brought out the same shade of pink on her cheeks. Did women plan these things? Her knees were pressed together, a pad of paper on her lap. She tried to smile, then gave up. She was the same petite, freckled brunette who had left his brother at the altar five years ago…and Chance wasn't entirely blameless in that, either. Her hair was longer now—tousled curls that tumbled around her shoulders—and she rose halfway and put out her hand.

"You're back," he said woodenly, taking her hand. He'd meant to give her a perfunctory shake, but he didn't let go in time, and she tugged her fingers free.

"Close the door, would you?" Mayor Scott said, and Chance swung it shut behind him without looking back. It closed louder than necessary, and he shot the mayor an incredulous look. Chance didn't like surprises—especially the personal kind—and the mayor knew exactly how personal this was. The entire town of Comfort Creek knew—they'd all been at the wedding that didn't happen.

"Now, I know there's a bit of history between you," the mayor went on quickly. "I'm trusting we can get past that. I've hired Miss Jenkins to be the events coordinator for the remembrance ceremony."

Sadie had left town five years ago on the morning she was supposed to marry Chance's brother, Noah. Chance hadn't forgiven her for that disappearing act yet.

"Are you serious, sir?"

"She comes highly recommended," the older man replied. He pulled out a wad of tissues and wiped his nose. "She also has a wealth of experience."

Chance glanced over at Sadie, eyeing her for a moment. He was angry—that was easier to deal with than the more complex emotions swarming beneath the surface. Because in those five years, she hadn't contacted him… not that she owed him anything, exactly. He shouldn't have gone to her house the night before the wedding. He shouldn't have stood with her on the porch, talking late into the evening. He shouldn't have reached out and touched that tendril of hair that hung down her neck…

"We're all professionals here," the mayor went on, his tone chilling noticeably. "I'm sure we can get a job done. You two will need to work together."

Mayor Scott was Chance's boss, and Chance didn't actually get to quibble over whom the mayor hired for event planning. He knew that, he just couldn't believe that of all people to choose, the mayor would choose the woman who had broken his brother, Noah's, heart—the reason Noah had been so eager to join the army. No one knew the truth, though, that before Sadie took off, Chance had almost kissed her. And he suspected that if it weren't for that moment of weakness, if he hadn't confused her, she might have gone through with the wedding and Noah might still be alive. Noah's death was utterly senseless. He'd left Comfort Creek to go lick his wounds, and while he was stationed overseas, he'd been shot in a routine exercise by friendly fire. Where was the meaning in that?

"Chief?" Both Mayor Scott and Sadie were looking at him now. He'd been silent for a few beats, and he inwardly grimaced.

"Yes, sir, of course," Chance replied with a nod. "We're all professionals."

"Great." The mayor beamed one of those politically golden smiles of his, and folded his hands in front of him. "Because this remembrance ceremony is important to our entire town. These young men were ours, and we are forever indebted to them for the freedom we enjoy. I want this ceremony to reflect our gratefulness, and our respect. Comfort Creek sent them out with fanfare, and we will never forget—" The older man's voice cracked, and he cleared his throat, and blinked back a mist of tears. "I know you feel the same."

Mayor Scott had three pictures around the office of his son, Ryan, ranging in age from his first day of kindergarten to him as a fully grown man in army dress uniform. Chance had the same kinds of photos around his home: the picture of him and his brother as kids, arms around each other's shoulders as they squinted into the camera on some family vacation; the snapshot from his graduation from police academy where his brother was giving him a noogie; the picture of Noah in army uniform, duffel bag at his feet. It was hard to encapsulate an entire person in a few pictures, but he'd tried nonetheless. It was as if the pictures helped to hold those memories together, remind the world that this man had mattered.

"I appreciate this opportunity, Mayor Scott," Sadie said. "We'll put together a program that honors these men and their families. You've lost more than we can comprehend, sir."

"So has Chance," the mayor said with a nod. "Ryan and Noah, Terrance and Michael—they all deserve to be remembered." He glanced at his watch. "I apologize for doing this, but I have a meeting in about ten minutes with the ladies complaining about noisy garbage collection." He tapped a pen on a pad of paper. "So let's meet next week and see where we are. I've already gone over some of my expectations with Miss Jenkins, and I'm sure she can fill you in, Chance."

So that's where things stood—the mayor was now planning this event with Sadie. While he'd never been keen on doing this ceremony, he didn't like being squeezed out, either.

Chance rose and gave a curt nod. "I'm sure she can."

He hoped his dry tone wasn't as obvious to them as it was to himself. Sadie gathered up some papers and tucked them into a leather bag, then rose, too.

"Thank you, sir," Sadie said with a smile, but it slipped when she saw Chance's expression. Her hazel gaze met his for a split second, and then she looked away. He could tell that he was making her uncomfortable, but she didn't deserve all the blame.

"We'll talk later, sir," Chance said with a sigh, then pulled open the door and gestured for Sadie to go ahead of him. He wasn't a complete Neanderthal.

Chance shut the door behind him, and as he passed Brenda's desk, she mouthed "sorry" at him. She'd known exactly what had been waiting for him in there, and she hadn't given him any warning. It wasn't her fault, though. Like Sadie, apparently, her loyalties were with the man who paid her. He gave her a small smile and tapped her desktop lightly with this tips of his fingers in reply as he walked past. It wasn't full-out forgiveness, just acknowledgment of her tough position.

They paused at the coatrack and took their coats. She had a gray, woolen dress coat that came to her knees, and she pulled a pink scarf from the pocket and wrapped it around her neck twice. All without looking at him. Sadie passed in front of him out of the office and her low-heeled boots echoed against the tile-floored hallway. She didn't say a word as they made their way back down the wooden staircase side by side.

When they reached the bottom, she turned toward him.

"It's good to see you, Chance," she said quietly, but her voice still carried through the empty halls.

"Is it? I got the feeling you didn't want to see me again." He couldn't say that he was glad to see her in the least, because he wasn't. He was supposed to be getting over her, not stepping back into that mire of emotion. However, the last thing Chance needed was to have everyone in the town hall listen to this conversation. "Let's go outside to talk," he said, gesturing toward the main doors. She nodded her agreement, and he opened the door to let her pass in front of him into the cold, winter air.

Sadie was still cute—why did he have to notice that? She came up to just past his shoulder and the scent of her perfume brought back a flood of memories. Sadie's laugh, Sadie's jokes, the way Sadie used to tip her head onto Noah's shoulder, and how Chance's insides had roiled with jealousy. His twin brother's fiancée had been out of his league from the start. She was the woman that Chance had measured all others against...except he hadn't intended to ruin his brother's happiness, or chase his brother's bride out of town.

Chance followed her out the door, then stopped on the sidewalk. She turned back, green-flecked eyes meeting his with irritation. She hitched her bag up on her shoulder.

"So you still won't forgive me?" she asked. "It's been five years!"

"He died, Sadie." There was no making this up to Noah. His brother was gone, and they were both to blame for that.

"Would you have rather I'd married him?" she demanded.

Sadie stepped back as a woman in a puffy green coat passed them and disappeared into town hall. She pasted a smile onto her face, hoping that it covered the rising emotion inside of her. Someone in a pickup truck called, "Morning, Chief!" as the vehicle rumbled past. There was no privacy on the streets of Comfort Creek.

She'd been afraid to come back because she knew that she'd let down the entire Morgan family. When Noah had proposed, he'd had the thrilled support of his brother and parents. She knew some women who married men whose families hadn't been terribly thrilled about the wedding, but that hadn't been her experience with the Morgans. They'd welcomed her with open arms. Her rejection of Noah would have felt like a rejection of all of them. But how could she marry Noah when she'd experienced more in one unfortunate moment with his brother than she'd ever felt for Noah?

But she'd come back to Comfort Creek anyway, because while she'd dashed out on her wedding, she didn't want to be the kind of woman who ran away from conflict. Comfort Creek was her home, too, but standing here on Birch Street with a lump in her throat wasn't exactly how she'd hoped to do this.

"Let me buy you a coffee at the diner," Chance said. "It's cold out here." He met her gaze, at least. Lucy's Diner was just down the street by the highway, walking distance from town hall.

"Alright," she agreed.

Sadie had expected this to be difficult. When her grandmother told her that Mayor Scott needed an events planner, the timing was perfect—for her at least. At that point, she hadn't realized that the event would be a commemorative ceremony for her ex-fiancé. That was uncomfortable, to say the least. Was she the right person for the job? Would Comfort Creek be angry or supportive? But the mayor assured her that he didn't see a conflict of interest. He needed a qualified event planner, and he trusted her to have the right "feel" for the town.

When the mayor told her that she'd be working with Chance Morgan, she'd almost refused the job. She hadn't spoken to anyone but her grandmother since she'd left town, and she'd prayed long and hard about the job offer. But home was calling to her, and she felt as if this was what God wanted her to do. Still, before Comfort Creek could be home in every sense, she had to face the people she'd hurt and make her apologies. She'd have to face Chance, and that knot of emotion he'd caused inside of her… It wouldn't be easy, but when God pushed her forward into character growth, some pain was to be expected. She'd just hoped that God would have prepared some hearts before she arrived.

As they headed down the street, Sadie evaluated Chance out of the corner of her eye. He was still the same tall guy she remembered, but he looked stronger, somehow. Maybe he'd bulked up a little—could that be it? Or just a few years more life experience. He was police chief now—that was a considerable step up in his career. He'd been up for the position just before the wedding, so this shouldn't be a surprise. But the years seemed to have aged him. There were lines around his eyes that hadn't been there before, and his sandy-blond hair was turning silver at the sides. But he was only thirty-eight—six years older than her. Stress, maybe? In every other way, he was the same old Chance—tall, fit, serious. They'd been close back then, but by the look in his eye now, all that was in the past.

"You really think you're the one to plan a ceremony in Noah's honor?" Chance asked, interrupting her thoughts.

"No, I think you are," she countered. "But Mayor Scott says you've fought him every step of the way."

"And that's my prerogative. You didn't even show up for the funeral."

Sadie heard the resentment in his voice.

"I didn't think it would be right to come to the funeral," she replied. "After I left the way I did."

"Maybe you were right."

"I sent your parents a sympathy card, though." She'd spent an hour standing in a card shop looking for the right sentiment. She'd been heartbroken, too, when she heard about Noah's death. She'd loved him—even if marrying him would have been a mistake. The world had been a better place with Noah in it.

"I saw it."

His tone was still wooden, and irritation simmered inside of her. What had he expected her to do? She wasn't part of the family. She was probably the least favorite person of the Morgans in general. Showing up at the funeral would have been in bad taste—it would have drawn attention away from Noah and put her into the spotlight. But more than that, was she supposed to stay away indefinitely? Comfort Creek didn't belong to Chance Morgan; he wasn't the only one to have grown up here.

"Chance, it's been five years." She eyed him cautiously. "I'm sorry about the way I handled things, but marrying Noah wasn't going to work. I should have figured it out sooner, but I didn't. I couldn't marry him."

"Ending things would have been fine," he retorted. "But you didn't face him. You didn't explain anything. You just walked out. We all showed up at the church, and I stood next to my brother at the front, waiting for you to come down the aisle. It was a full forty-five minutes before your grandmother arrived and told us you weren't coming. Do you know what that did to him? Do you know what it's like to get that kind of news in front of a church full of family and friends?"

Sadie felt that old swell of guilt—she'd lived with it every day since she'd run away from her wedding. She'd been dressed in that beaded gown, her veil already affixed to her updo. She'd been putting on her shoes, ready to go to the church when she caught a glimpse of herself in the mirror and it all came crashing in on her. She couldn't be Mrs. Noah Morgan. She'd thought that what she'd been feeling for her fiancé's brother was a crush—something that would pass. Then, on that porch the night before, he'd admitted to having felt the same thing for her...

The right thing would have been to go down to the church and explain it in person, but she knew herself—she might have walked down that aisle anyhow, just to keep everyone happy, and she couldn't risk that. So she'd changed into a pair of jeans, grabbed her suitcase that was already packed for a Caribbean honeymoon, and called a cab. Nana assured her that she'd explain.

"I'm sorry," Sadie said. "But there was no kind or easy way to call off a wedding the morning it was supposed to happen. I made my peace with that a long time ago. At least I didn't marry him and break his heart after two kids and a mortgage."

Lucy's Diner was located at the corner of Birch Street and the highway, an old brick building with a red roof and a large sculpture of a bull that stood between the highway traffic and the parking lot. Lucy's Diner had been in that exact spot for the last sixty years, when Comfort Creek was nothing more than a gas station, a church and a grain elevator, and as they approached the front door, Sadie heaved a sigh. This was past the point of discomfort, and the last thing she wanted was to sit in a diner and rehash old hurts.

"Do you really want that coffee?" she asked as they stopped in front of the diner. "We could do this another time. No pressure."

"Of course, there's pressure," he retorted. "We have to work together. We have a deadline."

He was right about that. Chance pulled open the door and stepped back. What was with him and those perfect manners? He'd always been like this—proper, disciplined, always the cop. She sighed and walked into the warmth, then headed toward a booth in the back. He followed, accepting a couple of menus from the waitress on his way past.

Once they were settled with glasses of ice water in front of them and their coats piled beside them, Chance leaned forward in his chair.

"I have to ask this—" Chance swallowed. "Was it because of me? I was out of line that night on the porch. I shouldn't have confused you like that. I should have—"

"Confused me?" Sadie shook her head. "You make me sound like a half-wit. I wasn't confused or in a muddle, Chance."

His face colored, but he'd hit a nerve there. That was a question she'd asked herself a hundred times since. Had she dumped Noah because of Chance? Was that moment of butterflies and tenderness enough to unhinge a five-year relationship with a good man?

"I just..." Her stomach had flipped. Her breath had caught. She'd stared up into Chance's blue eyes and she'd felt weak in the knees—none of which she'd ever felt for Noah. But there was no way she could confess that to Chance.

"It wasn't because of you," she said, and that was the truth. "Noah and I weren't strong enough together. That's all."

She'd wanted what Noah had to offer. He was a carpenter who was doing very well for himself in Comfort Creek. He had a large ex-

tended family who were close and supportive. He'd already built their future home on
an acreage outside of town. He'd offered her
everything she thought she wanted…

The waitress arrived just then, and Chance
ordered a coffee and a piece of pie.

"Just coffee for me, thanks," she said with
a tight smile.

The waitress left them in peace once more
and Sadie fiddled with the napkin-wrapped
cutlery in front of her. She'd been to this diner
countless times over the years, but the first
visit that she could remember had been with
her nana.

At the age of eight, her mother had brought
her to Comfort Creek to visit Nana for a few
days. That night, Sadie watched from the up-
stairs window of Nana's house as her mother
loaded a suitcase into the back of her musician
boyfriend's car. She remembered being confused. Why was her mother outside at this time
of night? Why was Angelo here? Her mom
had looked up, seen Sadie in the window and
blown her a kiss. Then she'd hopped into the
front seat and the car roared off.

No one blew a kiss and left forever, but that
was what Mom had done, and that was how
her life with Nana had begun. The next morn-

ing, Nana had brought her to the diner for a special breakfast, and she'd laid it out for her. Mom had gone away. Nana would take care of her from now on.

So Comfort Creek was home—the only home she had—and if Chance thought she'd stay away because they had some complicated history, then he had another think coming.

"I thought if I gave Noah some space, he could move on more easily. I owed him that much, at least."

"He didn't," Chance said.

Noah only died a year ago, so he'd had enough time to move on. He would have been one of the most eligible men in Comfort Creek. He would have had his pick of women...especially after what Sadie had done to him.

"There must have been girlfriends..." she said.

"Nope."

Her heart sank. "I know I hurt him, but—"

"It more than hurt him. It crushed him, Sadie." Chance's voice was low. "He wasn't the same after that."

And then he'd joined the army. Was Chance blaming *her*? Noah had mentioned an interest in the army before they got engaged, but she had no interest in being a military wife, and he'd let it drop. She'd assumed that was the end of it.

"I didn't know he'd do that," she said, hoping he'd believe her. "I thought I was doing us both a favor. I thought he'd move on with Melissa Franco or Melanie Brooks." Both women had been halfway in love with Noah, throwing themselves in his path every chance they got.

The waitress arrived with a coffeepot and the slice of pie. She poured them each a steaming cup.

"Anything else I can get for you two?" she asked.

"No, thanks." Chance's tone was curt, and the waitress retreated. "So why are you back, then? I thought you'd made your life in Denver."

Sadie's gaze wandered toward the window— the familiar stretch of highway, the faded sign out front promising the county's best burgers next to the black-painted sculpture of the bull with its horns down. A dusting of snow fell from the gray sky.

Sadie dragged her gaze back to Chance and smiled sadly. "I wanted to come home."

And maybe Comfort Creek wouldn't be the respite that she'd imagined it would. She'd wanted the comfort of Nana's advice and home cooking. She'd wanted to come back to the only place that knew her—the good and the bad. She wanted to settle down, not with a man, but on her own terms.

"And you're starting up a business, I take it," Chance added.

"Yes," she said, grabbing a sugar packet and tearing it open. "I am. Mayor Scott is being very supportive. He has friends who need a good event planner, and his daughter, Trina's, wedding is coming up. I have a good chance of making a go of this here. In Denver, I was working with a big event planning firm and I got some great experience."

"And if you do well with this remembrance ceremony, he'll pass your name around with a glowing recommendation," Chance concluded.

"Something like that." That was how businesses got started—word of mouth. This was a priceless opportunity. If she was going to support herself here, she needed the boost. She stirred the sugar into her coffee.

"So basically, you're back to make some money," he concluded.

"That isn't even fair!" Her anger sparked to life. "I need to make a living. What do you expect me to do? I'm good at this, Chance. I've got some great experience, and I really think I have a lot to offer Comfort Creek. So yes, I need to make a living, and yes, I want to grow my business and succeed. What's so wrong with that?"

He heaved a sigh, then shook his head. "Nothing. I hope it works out for you."

Did he really? She wasn't so sure. But a single woman didn't have the option of laying low if she wanted to support herself, so if Chance didn't like seeing her around town, he'd have to sort out his feelings on his own. She was tired of feeling guilty. She deserved a fresh start as much as anyone.

"Chance, I'm asking you—" She paused, unsure how to say this. "I get that you're mad at me, and I know that we won't be friends like we were before…but I'm here. And we have to work together. I just need to know if that's going to be possible."

In fact, it would be better if they weren't friends like before. Those lines had blurred, and there wasn't an easy way to recover from that. At least not for her.

"Of course," he said, and for a moment, his gaze softened. "Like the mayor said, we're all professionals." He slid the plate of pie toward her, then grabbed his coat from the bench beside him. "It's on me. I remember you liked pie." Then he rose to his feet and tossed a bill onto the table. "Come by my office Monday morning—let's say nine—and we'll get to work."

"Alright." She nodded. "Thank you. I'll be there."

Chance turned and walked away, leaving Sadie alone at the table with a piece of strawberry-rhubarb pie and a cup of untouched coffee. Not exactly the welcome she'd been hoping for, but it was a start.

Chapter Two

Sadie was back in town. Chance rolled that fact over in his mind while he drove toward the police station. If it weren't for the timing of this commemorative ceremony, he might not be so raw about the whole thing, but as it was, all those memories crowded just beneath the surface, and it had only been a year since Noah's death. He'd been praying for God to help him to heal, but so far, those prayers had gone unanswered.

And he needed healing from more than just his brother's death; he needed to let go of those feelings for Sadie. He'd thought he had, but when he saw her again today, it came crowding back in—that same unwanted attraction to Sadie and a flood of guilt.

He was the chief of police, and ran a sensitivity training program here in Comfort Creek—

he wasn't supposed to be the one struggling with personal issues. He was supposed to be the guy with the answers. How come every time he prayed for strength, he ended up driven to his knees? If anyone had asked him yesterday if five years had made a difference, he'd have said yes, it had. A lot had changed. But today, looking Sadie in the face, it was as if those years had melted out from under him.

The heat in his cruiser pumped into the car, and he reached over and turned it down. Sadie was back, and by the sounds of it, she wanted to make this permanent. He knew that he'd played a part in her run for Denver, but he'd been willing to talk about it. He could have told her that it was one moment of weakness, and that he could curb his feelings and she'd never be faced with them again. Had she stayed to talk about it. But she hadn't. She'd run. And now she was back and all was supposed to be forgiven, and he couldn't do it. The anger was back, and he couldn't just push it aside.

A fully planned wedding didn't evaporate, and it had taken weeks to help his brother handle all the details—clean up, return gifts, move her things back out of Noah's house. The entire time, his brother had been a walking shell of a man. He'd been hollow, wan, brittle. Sadie might have been able to just walk away, but Noah had to stay and deal with the fallout. And all that time, Chance had kept his secret and never told his brother what he'd done. He regretted that now. He'd never imagined that he wouldn't have a chance to get it off his chest.

Chance remembered the afternoon when Noah had told him his plans to join the army.

You can't just leave, Chance had protested. *You and I were going to buy that boat together, I thought.*

They had plans for the future—the Morgan brothers. They were going to buy a boat, then buy a little cottage by a lake and spend every weekend from April through October fishing.

I don't have anything left here, Noah had replied.

You have your entire life here!

And he had—Noah had run his own successful carpentry business. He had built a beautiful home on an acreage about twenty minutes outside of town, and he had his extended family all right there. This was the life he'd offered to share with Sadie, and there were several other women who'd immediately perked up at the news of the wedding that didn't happen. Noah didn't have to leave. What Chance should have said was, "You have *me* here, Noah."

Noah had been a wreck, and he'd said that the best way forward was through. Chance would have agreed, except *through* meant something different to Noah—it led to the army. He'd gone on one deployment, and the night he came back, Chance could see that his brother had changed. Of course, a year in Afghanistan would have an impact, but it was more than the tan and the ropy muscle. It went deeper, to the steely glimmer in his eye. Then he left for another tour, and the distance between the brothers grew more pronounced. And then there was a third tour that Noah never came back from.

Chance pulled into the parking lot next to the Comfort Creek Police Department. It was a squat, brick building on Main Street, right across the street from the bank. A large elm tree grew just beside it, branches blanketed with snow.

This sleepy town was the location of Larimer County's sensitivity training program. The cops who came here needed soft skills—patience, self-control and character growth. They didn't come to face off with criminals, they came to do just the opposite, actually, and face their own issues. Comfort Creek had plenty of space and quiet to do just that, and

Chance took his training program incredibly seriously. For the most part, these were good cops struggling with problems larger than they were, and Chance could sympathize with that. He knew what it was like to make one wretched mistake and watch his brother disintegrate because of it. A mistake didn't have to define a man, but all too often it did.

Sadie's face was still swimming through his mind as he trotted up the front steps to the police department. Her return had shaken him more than he liked to admit. He saw her grandmother, Abigail Jenkins, on a pretty regular basis. He'd have thought Abigail would give him a heads-up, but apparently he was wrong again. The women here seemed to have their own agendas that didn't include keeping him in the know.

Chance pulled open the front door of the station and was met with the familiar scent of coffee and doughnuts, and the low hum of the officers working at their desks.

"Chief, your newest trainee is waiting." Cheryl Dunn, the receptionist for the department, handed him a folder. She was about forty, slim, pale and efficient. She had three school-aged kids who called for her on a pretty regular basis, but she got the work done, and that was what mattered to Chance.

Trainees didn't usually arrive on a Friday, but he could be flexible. Besides, if he got this trainee sorted out before the weekend, it would free up his morning to meet with Sadie.

"Thanks, Cheryl." He flipped through the pages—signed forms, ID, that sort of thing. He was familiar with his newest trainee already. His name was Toby Gillespie, and he was being given this extra training because he was inflexible and generally intimidating to the public. The other officers nicknamed him Bear.

That had been Noah's nickname, too… Well, they'd called him Teddy Bear, and it was bestowed upon him by the girls in school for very different reasons—he gave good hugs, and despite his muscular physique, he was gentle with those smaller than him. Noah had been the all-American boy growing up. He was athletic, good-looking and got top grades. He played on the high school football team. He'd been dark haired and swarthy compared to Chance's sandy-blond hair and blue eyes—as different in appearance as they were in personality. Noah was a tough act to follow for a twin brother who had to study hard for mostly Bs and lacked that easy charismatic charm his brother emanated without even trying. It made for a complex dynamic between them, and if Chance had to be honest, he'd been jealous of Noah. And yet at the same time, he'd also been just as enamored with him as the rest of the town. Noah was like that—when he turned his attention onto a person, they couldn't help but love him.

Including Sadie...until the end, of course.

A uniformed officer sat in a chair in front of Chance's office. He wasn't tall, but his build was stocky, and he was muscular. Toby Gillespie obviously spent a lot of time in the gym, and Chance guessed the guy drank protein shakes for breakfast.

"Toby, I take it?" Chance asked.

Toby rose to his feet and stood at attention. "Good morning, sir."

"Come on in." Chance opened his office door and gestured to the chair opposite his desk. "Make yourself comfortable."

Toby stepped inside and stood beside the chair rigidly.

"At ease, officer. Have a seat."

The younger man visibly deflated and sank into the chair. None of his trainees liked being here—he was used to that. This was discipline, after all. Chance shut the door and went around to his own chair and flipped open the folder.

"You started out as military, right?" Chance asked.

"Yes, sir. Four years of army service, three deployments."

That was pretty close to Noah's service.

"And you've been on the force how long now?"

"Another four years, sir."

"Do you know why you're taking sensitivity training?" Chance asked.

"I'm too by-the-book, sir." Toby shook his head, and a look of disgust shone through that granite expression for a split second. "But the law's the law."

According to Officer Gillespie's commanding officer, Toby was intimidating to the public and no amount of coaching seemed to change that.

"Do you like desk work?" Chance asked.

"No, sir. Hate it." Toby arched a brow. "And yes, I know that's where I'm headed."

Chance had an idea of how to help this young officer, but it meant embracing this remembrance ceremony—something he'd been fighting ever since the mayor brought it up to him several weeks ago. There was no getting around it—Sadie had already been hired, and as police chief, he should have a role in it, too. Being a community leader didn't mean he always got to do what he wanted, but right now, he could see that this commemorative ceremony might be of use to more than just their own.

"Considering that you're ex-military, I have something I want you to help us with," Chance said.

"Yes, sir."

"We're working on a ceremony for Comfort Creek that is going to commemorate four young men who died in service. I want you to help us with that."

Toby froze, then shook his head. "Do I have a choice, sir?"

"Absolutely." Chance smiled amiably. "There is a room full of binders about feelings and appropriate reactions to them in the basement. You have two weeks with us, and I'm sure you could work your way through fifteen or twenty of those binders in that amount of time."

Toby looked away, his jaw tensing. He was doing the mental math there—how much could he endure, and which avenue did he prefer?

"I don't like rehashing my military days, sir," Toby said. "The past is the past. I'm a civilian now."

Toby was no civilian in his head, or in his demeanor. He was still acting like the soldier.

"Understood." Chance shrugged. "I'll get an

officer to show you down to the basement, then. You can get started today. I've got your first binder waiting on the table there. You can't miss it. There are some workbooks that go along with it, and we'll need full written responses that will be sent for psych evaluation—"

"I didn't say I wouldn't help out with your commemorative ceremony, sir," Toby said quickly. "I just said that I didn't want to dig into my own military service, if it's all the same."

Chance paused, watching conflicting emotions flit across Toby Gillespie's face. He was a good cop—most of the officers who ended up here were. He was the cop you wanted to cover you going into dangerous territory. He was a veritable tank who just needed to figure out how to disarm himself from time to time.

"I can tell you what it would entail," Chance said. "I need you to speak with the family members of the fallen men and get some personal information about them—pictures, military ranks and any medals they might have been awarded…that sort of thing. Bring that information back to me, and we'll talk."

Toby frowned. "That's not normally my strength—grieving families and all that."

No one liked facing grief, especially their own. Chance knew that better than anyone.

"It would be good practice with letting down your guard a little bit," Chance said. "But I'm not sending you in without some preparation. One of the men who died was my brother. You can practice with me."

Toby cleared his throat and looked down. "I'm used to interviewing suspects, sir, so talking with them isn't an issue. It's just that I don't tend to...come across right. Normally those kinds of assignments are saved for officers with a softer touch."

"That's what we're working on here," Chance said frankly. "The softer touch."

"So, if I did this—"

"No binders." This was an option he gave nearly all his trainees, and 95% of them chose to avoid the binders. There was something about county-approved sensitivity training that rubbed just about every officer the wrong way.

A smile flickered at the corners of the younger man's lips. "Fine. I'll do the interviews with the families. But if they complain about me—"

Chance had hoped that he'd agree, and not only because it would be of service to the community right now. Toby Gillespie was behaving like a military man, and it wasn't working with the police force. There was a certain amount of discipline and respect for command authority that the two careers had in common, but Officer Gillespie was suffering from something that had happened in the military—at least that was Chance's best guess—and it was bleeding into his work on the force.

"You'll start with me, remember? It'll be fine. In the meantime, you'll be assigned a cruiser and you can start patrol."

Chance didn't want to grieve for his brother with an audience, but sometimes helping a good officer get over his own issues meant a certain amount of vulnerability.

Lord, I hate this, he admitted silently. *I asked You to help me heal, and now everything seems to be about Noah all over again.*

He didn't want to face this, but it didn't look like he'd have a choice. He'd prayed that God would help him to work through his own grief, and sometimes when God answered a prayer, He did it with all the subtlety of a pile of bricks.

Sadie dropped her bag onto the seat of a kitchen chair and ran a hand through her hair. The meeting with the mayor had been more exhausting than she'd anticipated. There had been a very small and naive part of her that had been hoping that seeing Chance again would spark the old friendship they used to share, before those lines had blurred. Back when their relationship had been simple and sweet, she'd looked forward to seeing him, chatting with him, sharing jokes. Five years ago, Chance had been fun.

Marrying into a family that you honestly liked was a smart move, and that had been part of what had kept her moving toward the wedding. Mr. and Mrs. Morgan were kind and compassionate people—but they also knew how to stay out of a young couple's relationship. Chance had been a good friend, too, and she had pleasant memories of sitting in his cruiser on a summer day, her bare feet up on the dashboard as she chipped away at that serious shell of his.

Feet down, he'd say.

Make me, Officer. She'd shoot him a teasing smile, and he'd crack a smile at that point—possibly imagining what it would take to get her to do as she was told. Personally, she thought he enjoyed the challenge.

She'd thought that flirting was safe—this was Chance, after all—but maybe she'd been naive about that, too. Because the day before the wedding, Chance had swung by her place to drop off some place cards that Nana needed for the reception. While talking on the porch, everything had changed…melted away into a foggy moment as their eyes met and the world faded away around them. He'd pushed a piece of hair away from her face, and as he did so, his eyes had locked on her lips, and she'd known that he was thinking about kissing her. She was an engaged woman, after all—she knew what that looked like. And he'd confessed his feelings.

I should have asked you out first, because watching you fall in love with my brother has been agony. I'm not saying I'm better for you than he is, I'm just— Never mind.

You what?

If you ever changed your mind about Noah, I'd be the first in line.

Her heart still lurched at the memory. In that moment, an innocent friendship with her future brother-in-law suddenly came into a new light. He obviously felt a whole lot more for her than she'd realized, and that moment had startled her awake in more ways than one. First of all, it made her realize that she'd never felt breathless and off balance with Noah. And second, she'd recognized that the life she'd agreed to wasn't going to be enough.

Sadie rubbed her hands together. Nana's

house was always a little cold. Old houses were like sieves in the winter, the warm air flowing out as fast as it was pumped in. The house was small and white, with pink shutters that Sadie had painted herself when she was about thirteen. It stood at the end of Sycamore Street, just down from Blessings Bridal Boutique. As a girl, Sadie used to walk past that shop and stare into the windows at elegant bridal gowns. Was that why she'd been so quick to accept Noah's proposal? But then, what girl didn't want a wedding? She couldn't let herself feel guilty about that. She'd been twenty-five when he proposed, not exactly a wisp of a girl, and she did want to settle down. She wanted a family, kids…

"So?" Nana prompted. She stood at the sink rinsing some dishes. Her hair was white and pulled back into a bun, and she wore a pair of pleated jeans and a faded blouse.

"I've got the job," Sadie confirmed.

"That's my girl." Nana turned off the water and reached for a dish towel to dry her hands. "When I spoke with Eugene, he was quite excited. Apparently, our chief of police has been digging in his heels somewhat—"

"Chance," Sadie corrected. "Our chief of police is Chance Morgan."

Everyone else might be used to calling him chief, but she couldn't bring herself to do it. He was Chance—the guy she used to tease and hang out with.

"Yes." Nana smiled wanly. "And how did that go?"

"Not as well as I'd hoped." Sadie poured herself a cup of tea from a cozy-covered pot on the counter. "He's not thrilled to be working with me."

"He took his brother's death hard," Nana said. "We all did, really. Noah was universally loved…" She winced. "I'm not trying to make you feel bad."

"I know, I know." Sadie sighed. Her grandmother had been on her side when it came to ditching her own wedding. Nana had seen the writing on the wall, too, apparently.

Nana hung the towel over the oven handle. "Chance wouldn't speak of you after you left. Not to me, not to anyone."

"Really?" Sadie frowned. "He was that angry?"

Whatever he'd felt five years ago for her seemed to be safely gone. All she'd seen in his face was resentment—and she probably deserved it.

"Angry, loyal to his brother, maybe even a little betrayed himself." Nana took another mug from the cupboard and poured it full of tea. "My point is, he's bound to have a few residual feelings."

"Residual feelings." Sadie chuckled and took a sip. Her grandmother had no idea. "I suppose you could call it that. I'm pretty sure he can't stand me. He wouldn't even stay to drink his coffee in my presence."

"He walked out on you?" Nana frowned. If there was one thing her grandmother couldn't abide, it was rudeness, but Chance didn't exactly count as rude. He was angry, obviously, and not thrilled to be working with her, but he'd always been so controlled, so proper. He was a cop to the core.

"After he paid for our coffee and bought me a piece of pie," Sadie admitted with a shake of her head. "Noble to the last. I'm meeting him tomorrow morning at his office so we can sort out a few details for this ceremony."

"That's good." Nana nodded. "You both need this."

"Do we?" Sadie asked with a wry smile. "I'm not so sure. I wish I could be working with just about anyone else right now."

"*He* needs this," Nana replied. "I think he's built you up in his head into something more than you are, and facing you again will bring it all back into perspective."

So she'd been Godzilla in his head, had she? That was rather ironic. Well, maybe it would be good for him to see her as she was—a woman with feelings. He'd been able to see the woman in her before...

"And me?" Sadie asked. "Why do I need this?"

"Because you need to forgive yourself," her grandmother replied. "At the end, I hope you two can make some peace. Move on. Stumble across each other in the grocery store and *not* dive for cover."

Sadie chuckled. Nana had her own way of seeing things, and it was generally right. If Sadie was going to make her life here in Comfort Creek, then she needed to find some common ground with her almost-brother-in-law. Comfort Creek was a small town, and there was no avoiding someone with whom she had some unfortunate history.

"How is your mother?" Nana asked, and tears misted her eyes. When Sadie left town, she'd gone to the city and spent the better part of three years trying to find her mother. She'd worked for the catering firm, but her dedication to finding her mother had been stronger than anything else. She wanted answers—a reason for a mother to simply walk away from her little girl. She'd eventually found her living in a dumpy apartment, and she looked decades older than she really was.

"The last I saw her, she asked for money. And I—" Sadie put down her teacup "—I said no."

"You had no choice, dear," Nana said. "She's an addict. She'll always ask for money, and when you give it to her, she'll buy more drugs."

"She pleaded." Sadie met her grandmother's gaze. "She begged for it, Nana. I went back home and cried."

Nana came around the table and wrapped her strong arms around Sadie, pinning her arms at her sides. These hugs—she'd come home for moments like this, where she wasn't alone and someone else hurt as badly as she did when it came to her mom. Sadie's mother had always been flighty. That was Nana's term for it. She'd bounced from boyfriend to boyfriend, from job to job. When she'd gotten pregnant with Sadie, she wasn't even sure who the father was—at least that was her claim. It was possible that she didn't like who the father was… She'd never really put down any roots, and the most security Sadie had ever known was right here in her grandmother's house. But Sadie was her mother's daughter, too, and she'd inherited that tendency to bounce from job to job, from goal to goal...

"Sadie." Nana pulled back and looked her in the face. "There was nothing you could do. If there were, I'd have done it already, I promise you that. Lori might be your mother, but she's my baby girl."

Sadie knew that, and she wasn't a child, either. She understood the way drugs wreaked havoc on a person's mind and body, but when she thought about all those years of waiting— hoping her mom would drive back into town as quietly as she'd left—it was both heartbreaking and infuriating to realize that her mom had been so close by all that time, and had never checked on her.

"Nana, I missed you." Sadie meant that with every atom in her being. She'd missed her nana, the stability, the security, the love. For Nana, Sadie had been enough. She just hadn't been enough for her own mom.

"I'm glad you're home." Nana patted her cheek. "Now, let me feed you. What would you like?"

That was always Nana's solution for every problem—pie, bacon and eggs, perhaps a nice thick sandwich. Nana was a phenomenal cook, and she used food like therapy. Unfortunately, when Sadie was upset about something, her stomach closed down.

"I'm not hungry, Nana," Sadie said with a small smile.

"Well…" Nana sighed, then shot Sadie a hopeful look. "I've made a few additions to the dollhouse…"

Sadie couldn't help the smile that came to her face. "Are you still working on it?"

"Dearest, I've been working on that dollhouse for ages. I wouldn't just stop. Come on, then. I'll show you the newest renovations."

Nana's dollhouse was located in "the craft room," which was a room too small for a bed, and since it had a window, it was also not suitable for closet space. Nana had turned this room into her crafting space, and it was therefore where the dollhouse sat on display. This dollhouse had been a formative part of Sadie's childhood. She'd spent hours just staring into the tiny rooms, soaking in every perfect detail. Nana's dollhouse was four stories of sky blue, Victorian elegance on the outside, but inside, the rooms were carefully decorated in a 1950s style. The house opened on hinges, so that even more rooms were available once the two back wings had swung out on either side. The center of the house had a staircase that led up to the very top floor—a tiny attic room with a cot and a rickety little dresser.

"What have you changed?" Sadie asked as she followed Nana into the study. It was a few degrees colder in that room, and the window had frost on the inside, too.

"Oh, this and that," Nana said. "You know how it is. I decided to put real linens on the beds last year. Do you know how difficult it is to make a fitted sheet for a doll bed? I also made some tiny block quilts—all authentic, of course."

"Of course." Sadie bent down in front of the display of tiny rooms. She reached out to finger a tiny quilt on the bed in the attic. "Nana, this quilt is lined—" She stared at the minute craftsmanship.

"I told you—authentic." Nana was pleased that she'd noticed—she could tell.

The funny thing was that seeing this dollhouse again felt like home in a deeper way than anything else in Comfort Creek. She'd spent so many solitary hours staring into these rooms, imagining the family that lived there, their dramas and quarrels, their victories and quiet Sunday evenings spent all together in the tiny sitting room in front of the fireplace…

The mother in this house never left. She doted over her offspring and cooked lavish meals in the kitchen. The father came home every day at the exact same time, and he picked up a tiny newspaper from the sideboard in the hallway. Any mess left about—like the toys on the children's bedroom floor—was carefully orchestrated to be attractive. This house was perfection, frozen in an imaginary time where nothing could go so wrong that it couldn't be set right again.

"I added a telephone in the kitchen." Nana pointed to a pale pink rotary phone on the wall. "I found that one at the bottom of a bin in the craft shop. Liz could see how excited I was, and she charged me double, I'm sure. Oh! And I've been working on making sure that every single book in the library is real. I've found a tutorial online for making books that open. I tried making them with four or five pages each, but they just fanned open. It was very annoying. So I used thick cardstock on both sides, so that each book opens to the center." Nana paused. "I was hoping you'd help me choose which books to include in the library. Maybe a few of your favorites, Sadie."

Sadie rose and shot her grandmother a look

of surprise. "Did you say you found a tutorial online?"

When Sadie left, Nana hadn't exactly been tech savvy. She could email, but she was a strict telephone chatter. There was no video chatting with Nana, and for the most part, she tended to stay pretty old-school.

"It's how it's done these days, dear." But her cheeks pinked in pleasure. "Okay, truth be told, last month, Ginny Carson's grandson showed me how the tutorials worked. So I'm still new at it."

"Ah." Sadie shot her grandmother a smile. "I'm still impressed."

"Welcome home, dear girl. Now you sit yourself down and get reacquainted with the old place, and I'll go sort out some supper."

Sadie was thirty-two, and this old dollhouse still soothed a part of her heart that nothing else could touch. This was the part of her that had softened to Noah—the part of her that longed for a perfect life with a picket fence. Noah had offered a picture-perfect existence here in Comfort Creek—a handsome man to come home to at the same time every day and pick up the paper off a sideboard table…

But it hadn't been enough, because she didn't love him enough, and she wasn't sure that she was the kind of woman who could stay content with so much monotony, anyway. In the real world, with real emotions, real hardships, the life Noah offered wasn't enough to fill her heart, after all. But he should have been, and if she'd been a little less like her flighty mother, he *would* have been. That knowledge had been nagging at her for the last five years. No man was perfect, and relationships didn't stay in the honeymoon phase. Noah, his house, his family, this town—it all *should have been enough*.

Nothing had ever been enough for Mom. No boyfriend. No job. No town. They'd bounced from place to place, from romance to romance for her mom. And no matter how nice the guy, her mother always found a reason to cut him loose and they'd leave again… No one had been enough to fill that hole in her mother's heart, and she feared that she might be the same. At least looking back on it all. She had been when it came to jobs around town.

If she could be faced with a sweet guy like Noah and the perfect life and still walk away from it all because she felt a rush of emotion with another man, maybe she deserved a life alone.

God rest Noah's soul.

Chapter Three

The coffee they made at the station was about as thick as boiled tar, but it was also concentrated caffeine, which the officers took strange pride in gulping down. Chance, however, appreciated a fine cup of coffee, and over the years he'd gotten more particular about how he liked it. He brewed his own at home and brought it in a thermos that no one was allowed to touch upon pain of traffic detail. He was sipping his own brew Monday morning as he headed through the bull pen toward his office.

"Chief, could I get a signature?"

Bryce Camden was their newest recruit to the Comfort Creek police force. He was newly married, his wedding ring still shiny, and he fiddled with it when his hands were free.

"How's Piglet?" Chance asked. Piglet was the nickname Bryce gave his adopted daughter—now eight months old—because of her dedication to finishing a bottle. They were all attached to that baby since she'd been dumped on the station doorstep as a newborn.

"Growing like a weed," Bryce said with a grin. "She's trying to say 'Dada'—I'm sure of it."

"Yeah?" Chance scanned the forms that Bryce handed him, and he jotted down his initials where required and signed the bottom, then handed them back. "Isn't it kind of early for that?"

"She's a genius, what can I say?" Bryce spread his hands and grinned. "I've got video proof on my cell phone, if you don't believe me."

"Later," Chance chuckled. "I've got a meeting to prepare for."

"Much later, then," Bryce said. "I'm just leaving on patrol."

Bryce had certainly settled into family life, and Chance felt a pang of envy. That was the goal, wasn't it? Beautiful wife, a couple of kids, a home with a woman's touch around the place… Somehow he'd managed to avoid the comfortable life all this time, and he was pushing forty. Part of it was that he hadn't met a woman who intrigued him enough to get married, and living in a town this small, there weren't a lot of fresh options. The other part of it was guilt. He and his brother hadn't had a lot in common—except their taste in women. The one woman to make him sit up and take notice had been his own brother's fiancée. There was a whole lot wrong with that.

Chance headed into his office and paused for a sip of coffee, then slid into his chair and turned on the computer. He had a fair amount of paperwork to get through today, plus there was the meeting with Sadie. He'd asked her to come by early so that he could get it out of the way and stop worrying about it. Sadie might have been the one woman to catch his attention over the years, but she was also at the root of his deepest grief, and his unresolved guilt. If she'd just stayed in the city…

There was a tap on his door.

"Come in." His tone was gruff, and he looked up as the door eased open to reveal Sadie. He glanced at his watch. Was it nine already? Almost. She was five minutes early.

"Good morning, Chance."

They weren't going to be hung up on formalities, apparently. She wore a pair of jeans this time, and a white turtleneck under a puffy red jacket. She had a tablet in one hand, a purse over her shoulder. He nodded her in, and she closed the door behind herself without being asked. She was right, though—the last thing they needed right now was an audience. This was awkward enough, already.

"Have a seat," Chance said, clicking his emails shut once more. "So how are you?"

"Do you really care?" Her tone was quiet, but her gaze met his in challenge. "I'm not used to being left at a table on my own."

Ouch. Yeah, he'd regretted that as he'd walked out, and he'd had the weekend to kick himself for it. He'd been frustrated and eager to get some breathing space, but he'd known it was the wrong call.

"I'm sorry about that," he said. "I thought I'd dealt with Noah's death, and it's all coming back on me again. I'm not at my best."

"Okay." She nodded. "I get it. I'm probably a reminder of the old days."

"Yeah, you could say that." She was reminder of a whole lot of frustration that he'd kept hammering down into the pit of his stomach over the years.

"So let's just get the work part over with—"

"So how much did the mayor tell you about my feelings toward this ceremony?" Chance planted his elbows on his desk.

"He mentioned you weren't keen on the

idea." She licked her lips. "Personality conflict, maybe?"

"We've never really gotten along. We grate on each other." He sighed. "I'll level with you—Mayor Scott wants this big personal ceremony, and I don't. My brother isn't a bit of sentimental propaganda. And I don't like private grief being offered up for public consumption."

"You aren't the only one who loved Noah," she countered.

"Including yourself in that?" he asked coolly.

Color rose in her cheeks. "I did love him, Chance. I wasn't some monster who took advantage of Noah. I loved him."

If she'd loved Noah like she claimed, she could have been kinder in her rejection of him.

"And you want this ceremony?" he demanded.

"I'm not talking about myself!" she snapped. "I'm talking about his friends, his cousins, his extended family. People in Comfort Creek loved him. You aren't the only one who lost him, you know."

"And they got to grieve for him—at his funeral. We've done the public display. It's enough already."

"What about the other families?"

Chance shook his head. "You see the stories

online—some heart-wrenching news spot that features the grieving family left behind from a soldier killed in the war. People love it—they gobble it up. They shed a tear in sympathy, post it on social media, feel like they've done the patriotic thing. It's entertainment."

"And you're afraid this ceremony is going to be used the same way."

"You think it won't?" he asked. "This isn't for the community. This is for the mayor. It's that simple."

Sadie ran her free hand through her hair, tugging it away from her face. She still had that smattering of freckles over her nose that made her look younger than she really was, and combined with her green-flecked eyes... he pulled his attention away from those details.

"I've been hired to put together a commemorative ceremony for the town," she said slowly. "I report to Mayor Scott—as do you, I believe. This isn't about what I want, or what you want, this is about my client. I don't have much choice."

"Yeah, I got that." He leaned back in his chair. This had been what Sadie had always been like—strong, focused. "This isn't personal to you, is it?"

"I can't give you an answer you'd like," she

retorted. "If I say yes, it is personal, you'll tell me I have no right to personal feelings after what I did to Noah. If I say no, it's just business, then I'm the heartless wretch."

She had a point, and he smiled wryly. He didn't want to be friends with Sadie again. Friends had to be able to trust each other, and he didn't trust Sadie as far as he could throw her.

"Yesterday, you said we needed to be able to work together," she went on. "Do you still believe that?"

"Like I said, we don't have much choice."

"I won't take up more of your time than I have to." She pulled a business card out of her purse and slid it across his desk. "This is my cell phone number if you need to get in touch later on."

"Great." He took her card and tucked it into his front pocket, then passed her one of his own. "That's my number."

"Thank you." She tapped it against the desktop. "Should we get started, then? We'll need to decide on a musical style, both tasteful and evocative…"

Outside the office door, there was a scramble of feet, some raised voices and a bang as something large hit the floor. Chance jumped up and crossed the office in five quick strides. He hauled open the door and looked out.

Toby had a teenager in cuffs, and when the boy resisted, Toby nearly lifted him off his feet as he propelled him forward. Chance knew the kid—it was Randy Ellison. Chance knew better than to undermine his officers in public, but a quiver of irritation shot through him. Randy was all of sixteen, and he didn't need to be roughed up by the cops in his town; that wouldn't resolve a thing for the troubled youth.

"Officer Gillespie," Chance called. "What seems to be the problem here?"

"Consumption of alcohol under the legal age, public consumption, verbal abuse to an officer of the law, resisting arrest—"

Randy shot a baleful glare over his shoulder. "My brother-in-law's a cop, you know!"

Randy jerked his arm, and in response Toby simply raised the cuffs a couple of inches, and Randy froze as the pain hit his shoulder. Bryce Camden wasn't here, however; he was on patrol. Toby didn't seem fazed by the kid's attitude, and the only sign he showed of any kind of emotional response was a ripple in the muscle along his jaw.

Before Chance could decide on a course of action, Sadie pushed past him.

"Randy!" she exclaimed, marching across the bull pen. "For crying out loud, let go of him! You're going to dislocate his shoulder doing that!"

Sadie knew the Ellison boys from church. She used to help out with Sunday school before she got engaged, and she'd gotten to know Randy Ellison rather well. Back then, he'd been all of eight or nine, but under that rebellious shell there had been a very tender young heart.

The officer holding Randy's cuffed wrists eyed her with icy distance, and when Randy's gaze met hers, she saw the recognition.

"Miss Jenkins?" The attitude melted away, and he was just a boy again—albeit a boy who shaved now.

"Officer—" she looked at the name badge on the broad, wall-like chest "—Gillespie." She raised one brow and crossed her arms. "Let go of him. Now."

Chance came up behind her and put a solid hand on her shoulder.

"You aren't a commanding officer, Sadie," he said, his voice low. "Back down."

"Then tell him to get his hands off of Randy!" she snapped, turning to face Chance. She knew she was putting him in a difficult position, but she was tired of all this tiptoeing. This wasn't about her and Chase this time, it was about a kid who was being manhandled by an officer four times his size. It was outright bullying!

The officer lowered Randy's arms to a more comfortable position. It was something.

"Randy, are you okay?" she asked. "What's going on here?"

"Nothing, miss." Randy dropped his eyes to the carpet. She could smell the booze on his breath, and his eyes were a little glassy. She knew tipsy when she saw it. "My brother-in-law is a cop here...he'll help me out."

His brother-in-law... That's right, Lily Ellison had gotten married a few months back. Nana had told her about it. Sadie looked over at Chance, and his expression was about as icy as Officer Gillespie's. He nodded toward the muscular cop.

"Bring him to an interview room."

"Not a holding cell?" the officer asked.

"You heard me. An interview room. And..." He stepped closer to the man and lowered his voice. "Be a bit nicer, would you?"

Officer Gillespie blinked, then nodded, and nudged Randy toward a hallway.

"And you—" Chance's voice was tight, aloof.

"What?" she demanded. She regretted the

attitude that oozed out of her tone, but she was angry, and it couldn't be helped.

"You are not a police officer. You have no right to give orders in this station. I'm the boss here, and what I say goes. Don't you ever try and throw your weight around on my turf again."

Was he really intimidated by a woman half his size? She shook her head. "He was out of line, Chance!"

"He's my trainee to deal with," Chance retorted. "And that's *Chief Morgan*, to you."

The officers in the bull pen stared at them in silence, and she immediately saw her mistake. She'd been angry, and for some reason she was still having trouble seeing Chance as police chief around here. He'd never been boss when she knew him, and it looked like a whole lot more had changed than she'd realized. She swallowed hard, feeling the heat rise in her cheeks.

"I'm sorry," she said, lowering her voice. "It's just that I know Randy, and I know it's been a few years, but that boy has a good heart."

"We all know Randy," he retorted.

"That officer was about to break his arm!"

"Do you really think I'd let a teenager get roughed up on my watch?"

Perhaps not, but he wasn't listening to what

she was saying anyway. She knew this boy—
or she had known him—but that didn't matter
right now, at least not to Chance. It had been
a knee-jerk reaction, and it hadn't been her
stand to take. Except Chance had been taking
his sweet time in intervening—

"Now, if you don't mind, I have a kid to talk
with in the interview room." Chance turned to
the receptionist. "Call his mother at the grocery store. Tell her to come down to the station at her earliest convenience."

The receptionist nodded and immediately
picked up the phone, but not before casting
Sadie a sidelong look. She hadn't made any
friends here today, it seemed.

"Chance, I'm—" She swallowed the words
and started again. "Chief Morgan…" It wasn't
easy to use his official title. It changed things
between them—broadened the gap even more
than it already was.

"Yes?" His tone softened.

"I'm sorry for stepping on toes. It won't happen again."

Chance gave her a nod. "I appreciate that.
Now, I've got to deal with this, so we'll have
to reschedule our meeting. I'll call you."

He walked off briskly in the direction that
Officer Gillespie had taken Randy, and Sadie

turned back toward his office to collect her coat and bag. Chance was now police chief, and that changed more than she'd realized. They weren't equals, and while she used to be able to cajole Chance into good humor or make demands where she saw fit, that wasn't going to work anymore. There would be no more toes up on the dashboard of his cruiser, no more inside jokes between them. He was no longer her fiancé's twin brother, and he most certainly wasn't family. Chance was the commander of the entire force here in Comfort Creek, and he called the shots.

Working with Chance was going to be harder than she'd anticipated, because more than having to apologize for her actions five years ago, she'd also have to swallow her pride. Saying she was sorry was hard enough, but calling her old buddy "sir" would be a whole lot harder. And it looked like Chance wasn't going to make that any easier for her, either.

She buttoned her coat as she headed out the front doors of the station and didn't look back. She'd wanted a place to belong in Comfort Creek. She just hadn't counted on that position being lower than Chance Morgan's.

Chapter Four

Chance headed down the hallway toward interview room B. There were only two interview rooms, and room A was filled with file boxes. Chance paused at the door, looking into the sparse room at the young man sitting behind a bare table. His brown hair was shaggy, hanging down over his eyes in the style the teenagers seemed to like these days. He wore a baggy winter jacket that was unzipped to reveal a shirt with a band's logo on the front of it. He was slumped down in the chair, the cuffs off now that he was detained, and he rubbed idly at his wrists. Those cuffs had been tight.

Chance opened the door and stepped inside.

"Good morning," Chance said.

Randy was silent.

"A little early to be drinking, isn't it?" Chance asked.

"You mean my age, or before noon?" Randy quipped.

Chance wasn't amused. Killing off brain cells at his young age was nothing to laugh at. He pulled out the chair opposite Randy and sat down.

"Both, actually," Chance replied.

Randy looked away again. Chance knew Randy Ellison's family well. His older sister, Lily, had served as temporary foster care provider for the town for a few years, and she'd also married a cop from the sensitivity training program. Randy's mother was assistant manager at the local grocery store who worked long hours to provide for her kids. The Ellison boys had been getting more and more out of control as the years went by, and not because the town didn't care, either.

"You've got little brothers looking up to you," Chance said.

"So?"

"They do what you do," Chance replied. "You know that. Do you want them making your mistakes?"

Silence again. Chance could tell that he wasn't going to get anywhere this way. Randy was angry—very deeply angry—and appealing to the boy's honor wasn't going to suddenly fix that. Chance looked at his watch. It had been about fifteen minutes so far, and the grocery store wasn't far from the station.

"We're calling your mom. She'll be here anytime now, I'm sure."

Randy winced at that one, and Chance couldn't help the smile that twitched at the corners of his lips. Iris Ellison might have her hands full with these boys, but she hadn't given up on them yet.

"So what do we tell her?" Chance asked.

"What do you mean?" Randy frowned.

"I mean, according to Officer Gillespie, you were drinking alcohol and got mouthy. You're underage, you resisted arrest..." Chance crossed his arms over his broad chest. "Now, we can either tell her that you'll be facing charges in the youth courts, or we can tell her that we've come to another arrangement."

"What kind of arrangement?" Randy asked, his tone suddenly more contrite.

"Alcoholics Anonymous," Chance said. "I want you to start attending some meetings. They're held in the basement of the Hand of Comfort Church here in town on Tuesday evenings."

"I'm not an alcoholic..." Randy smiled tentatively. "I do some stupid things sometimes, but I'm not that bad. I can stop when I want to."

"You haven't stopped yet," Chance pointed out.

"Well…" Randy swallowed hard. "I could, though. And I will. I'll straighten up."

Chance had heard all of this before…from Randy and from other alcoholics. Randy's father had been an alcoholic, and he'd wrapped his car around a tree, so there was a bit of family history here. He knew what Randy wanted to believe, and he knew that the idea that he had a really big problem scared the kid. Sixteen wasn't very old. But now wasn't the time to go soft on him.

"I didn't ask if you thought you needed help." Chanced fixed him with a direct stare. "I asked if you wanted to be legally charged for your infractions or not."

Randy's face paled and he licked his lips. "Look, I'm really sorry. I shouldn't have been drinking. I just had this big fight with my mom this morning, and things have been tough lately, and—"

"A sorry isn't enough, Randy." Chance shook his head. "Once you're dealing with the law, you're officially past an apology. That stage is for dealing with your mom, not with a police officer."

"But Bryce—he'll tell you—"

"*Officer Camden* won't tell me anything I don't already know," Chance said. "And he's not the one who picked you up today, either. Bryce can't fix this, Randy."

Tears misted the young man's eyes, and he suddenly looked a whole lot younger. He pulled a hand through his hair and sucked in a wavering breath. Sixteen wasn't all that old from this side of things, but he could remember being Randy's age and thinking he could handle it all, too.

Chance could remember being sixteen when Noah made him promise to keep a secret about an overnight party he was going to attend complete with booze and eighteen-year-old cheerleaders. A seventeen-year-old friend of theirs ended up in the hospital with alcohol poisoning that weekend. They'd all felt so grown up until they had to dial 9-1-1 for an ambulance.

"Chief Morgan." Randy's voice held new respect. "You don't understand what going to AA meetings is going to do to me at school. The other guys… I mean, it'll stick a target on my back for every single meathead and jock in that place."

"It's called 'anonymous' for a reason," Chance replied. "No one talks about what happens in those meetings, and no one says who's there."

"Yeah, but in a town this size—"

"Randy." Chance's tone firmed. "I'm a busy man, and I'm not sitting here with you talking through the pros and cons about attending those meetings. This isn't negotiable. Either you give me your solemn word that you'll attend those meetings, or I will personally press charges that will land you in the juvenile court. We've had enough."

Randy's eyes widened, and he stared at Chance for a few moments.

Chance rose to his feet and pushed the chair back under the table. He leaned his broad palms on the back of the chair and eyed the young man questioningly. "So, what's it going to be?"

Randy nodded. "Okay. I'll go to them."

Chance was glad to hear that, not that he'd leave it up to a kid's word of honor, either.

"Now keep in mind that this is a legal requirement. If you don't attend those meetings from start to finish every Tuesday evening, I *will* press charges. The program facilitator will report to me when you arrived and when

you left every week. This is not a suggestion
or a good idea. You either comply, or we start
pressing charges. Are we clear on that?"

Randy nodded hurriedly. "Yes, sir."

"Excellent." Chance went to the door and
opened it. He glanced back at the young man
still slouched in that chair. "Randy, you can
be better than this," he added. "I know that
for a fact."

Randy didn't answer, and Chance stepped
out into the hallway and closed the door behind him. Officer Gillespie leaned against the
wall, apparently waiting for him to come out.
Toby immediately straightened when he saw
Chance.

"I'm sorry if I was too heavy-handed with
the youth, sir," Toby said, his voice low. "He
was belligerent and defiant. I thought I'd teach
him a little lesson. I apologize if I went too
far."

Chance angled his head toward the bull pen.
"Walk with me."

Toby fell into step next to him as they
headed out. The few officers who remained
at their desks stayed engrossed in their work.

"Randy Ellison's father was an alcoholic
who was killed in a car accident while under
the influence when Randy was four or five,"

Chance said. "Randy has three younger brothers and an older sister. Lily turned out just fine—she's married to a cop, actually. The other boys…" He shrugged. "They took after their dad, it seems. But their mother is widowed and works full-time-plus, trying to keep a roof over their heads and food in the cupboards. Randy's experienced a whole lot of discipline at school, and he's been bullied a fair amount, too. He doesn't need a heavy hand. He needs a solution."

Toby nodded. "I didn't know the backstory, sir."

"Nor could you be expected to," Chance replied.

"What is the solution?" Toby asked.

"Well, things have gotten out of hand with Randy Ellison over the last year, so I threatened to press charges," Chance went on. "We aren't doing him any favors letting him off with a talk and a warning. But if we press charges on this boy, it will change the course of the rest of his life."

"Maybe for the better," Toby said.

Chance shot the young officer a curious look. Since when did the inside of a jail help a kid back onto the straight and narrow? More often than not, the kid ended up traumatized and toughened—not a great combination.

"Most likely not," Chance said. "But we can't let him run wild, either. Now, our interest in Comfort Creek isn't just to maintain law and order, but to make sure that our kids get the best chance they can at becoming productive members of society. And sometimes that means getting creative."

"How creative, sir?" Toby frowned.

"We aren't pressing charges…yet. But he will be required to attend AA meetings for the next year in order to keep those charges at bay."

Toby nodded, silent.

"It isn't about control, Toby. It's about a solution."

"And the woman—" Toby nodded toward the front door. "The one you yelled at…"

Sadie. An image of her standing there, her eyes snapping fire and hands on her hips jumped to mind, and he pushed it back.

"I didn't *yell* at anyone," Chance retorted.

Toby didn't answer, but a twitch at the officer's eyebrow told him that he didn't agree with that. "Fine. The woman you reprimanded—"

"What about her?"

"How do you deal with that kind of interference from the public? At my level, I mean. Obviously, you can get away with a lot more."

A lot more? How exactly had he come across there?

"I didn't yell at her," Chance repeated, and he glanced over to see several officers looking at them. They turned quickly back to their computer screens as soon as they saw they'd been spotted.

"Permission to speak freely, sir," Toby said quietly.

"Granted."

Toby licked his lips. "I'm not questioning your judgment in that situation, sir. I'm simply asking how an officer at my level could effectively deal with an angry citizen without... scaring her, sir."

That was why Toby was here, wasn't it? He tended to intimidate the public and needed to learn that softer touch—which Chance *hadn't* used with Sadie a few minutes ago. Had he really shouted at her? He'd been mad, but he hadn't meant to intimidate...not really.

"Did she look scared?" Chance asked, lowering his voice further.

"She looked intimidated, sir," Toby said.

Great. That hadn't been his intention, exactly. He'd wanted her to back off and stop treating him like a buddy, but he wasn't the kind of man who took any pleasure in bullying a woman, either.

"Normally, you'd use polite language when dealing with an interfering citizen," Chance said. "You'd ask her to please step aside and allow you to do your job. You'd assure her that you will speak with her in a few minutes if she will just wait, and you maintain eye contact—it gets someone's attention better than a raised voice."

All advice Chance could have put to good use with Sadie.

"Got it, sir."

Chance sighed. "Okay. So if you could just wait here for Randy's mother. When she gets here, she's going to be upset. You can practice keeping your voice low, maintaining eye contact and using extreme politeness when speaking with her. Keep in mind that you are a physically intimidating man, and you want to make her feel safe with you. You'll want to tell her that in exchange for compliance with an AA program, we will delay any charges against her son."

"Yes, sir."

Toby still looked like a tank, but Iris could handle him. Besides, this would be some excellent practice. Guilt wormed its way up Chance's gut as he headed toward his office. He'd been frustrated with the entire situation, and that wasn't an excuse to take it out on Sadie. Chance was a big man, too, and he didn't like to use that to his advantage, especially when it came to a petite woman. And he hated that he'd stooped to that...especially in front of his sensitivity trainee.

Chance closed his office door and angled around his desk. He took the card Sadie had left with him earlier that morning out of his pocket and dialed the phone number. She picked up after two rings.

"Good morning. This is Sadie Jenkins."

"Sadie— Hi…"

"Chance?" She cleared her throat. "I mean, Chief. Hello."

"Chance is fine," he said with a sigh. "I wanted to apologize for earlier."

"Oh…" She sounded mildly surprised. "No, I was out of line. I'm sorry, too. I just got protective. I mean that officer— It's just the way he looks. He didn't seem to even recognize how much that would hurt, you know?"

Yeah, the exact reason Toby was here—to rectify that public image.

"Randy is fine," Chance assured her. "I've

spoken with him, and while I can't give you any details, we've got it all under control."

"Well…good. I'm glad. He was a good kid back then, Chance. I mean, a handful, but deep down, that boy has a good heart. I know it."

She sounded like the same old Sadie again, passionate, opinionated, direct. In some ways it was like no time had passed at all…and that made everything harder.

"We still need to discuss that commemorative ceremony," Chance said. "How about we do it on some neutral turf?"

"Such as?"

"Let's meet at The Daily Grind at noon. I'll buy you soup and a sandwich."

"Deal." He could hear the smile in her voice.

"And I'm sorry if I barked at you earlier. I probably could have handled that a little better. If I scared you, or—"

"You don't scare me, Chance." He could hear the eye roll in her voice. "I could take you on, any day."

Chance couldn't help laughing. "See you at noon."

"I'll be there."

He felt better as he hung up the phone. He might not like working with her, and he might not like that she was back in town, but he wasn't going to turn into some Neanderthal just because he was uncomfortable.

He was a better man than that.

Five years ago, The Daily Grind was only about coffee and some baked goods, but Sadie liked the addition of soup and sandwiches. Otherwise, the place looked the same—the few tables by the windows, the lending library bookshelf on the wall opposite the counter. It was strange coming home after such a long absence. Everything was the same, but different. Including her.

Reconnecting with her mother had been traumatic. Somehow, she'd carried a few daydreams with her, and when she finally saw her mother again, she'd had to let those go. Mom wasn't going to be a mature and loving presence in her life, no matter how much she longed for it. But she wasn't the same free spirit who drove away with her boyfriend all those years ago, either—she was harder, more broken. Casual drug use had solidified into relentless addiction. But Sadie had *seen* her mother. And she'd hugged her. That would have to be enough for now.

Sadie set her bowl of cream of mushroom soup on the table opposite Chance, then put her BLT sandwich down next to it. She hadn't realized how hungry she was until she smelled the food.

"This looks really good," she said as she got settled.

Chance had a bowl of minestrone soup and a cheese sandwich, and he waited until she was settled. They both bowed their heads for a silent grace. Hers consisted of a wordless lifting of her heart.

"So you said that Randy's doing okay?" she asked as she crumbled some saltines into her soup.

"His mom came by this morning and picked him up," Chance confirmed. "But I'm worried about that kid."

"So he's been getting into trouble." It still seemed hard to believe. Those boys had always been slightly wild, but they'd been good kids. Or at least she'd thought so.

"Over the last two or three years, he's gotten angrier," Chance said.

"How about the other three boys?" she asked.

"Burke is what…fifteen now? He's not as bad as his brother. He's actually started helping his sister with her bed-and-breakfast. He's running some errands for her, taking care of the yard, doing some of the heavy lifting. He's doing really well with some responsibility. Bryce, the cop Lily married, has really taken Burke under his wing. As for the twins, they look up to Randy a lot, which isn't ideal. He hasn't been a great influence on them."

Carson and Chris Ellison had been identical rascals when she'd known them. Loud, boisterous, but with the biggest blue eyes she'd ever seen. She used to take great pleasure in dressing them up as angels for the Christmas pageant every year…even if they were the noisiest angels to ever step foot on the stage.

"They were in kindergarten when I taught them Sunday School," she said, taking a bite of creamy soup.

"Eighth grade is a lot less adorable," Chance said with a small smile.

The front door opened and shut, the bell overhead tinkling. Sadie glanced up to see Ralph Harrison come into the shop. He was an older rancher, who owned about eight hundred acres of cattle ranch land nearby. He wore polished cowboy boots, and his blue checked shirt was tucked into his jeans. Ralph glanced at the counter where the girl was waiting to take his order, and then he spotted Chance and he headed in their direction.

"Howdy, Chief," Ralph said with a nod. "Good to see you."

"You, too, Ralph."

The men exchanged a few pleasantries, and Sadie listened in silence. Ralph Harrison was a wealthy rancher who didn't defer to many, but she heard the note of respect in his gravelly voice when he'd addressed Chance. And Chance spoke with Mr. Harrison like an equal. Five years ago, there'd been a pretty large gulf between the two men socially. That gap seemed to have closed. They finished up their short conversation and the older man tipped his hat politely at Sadie.

"Ma'am," he said with a nod, and then headed back over to place his order. Sadie watched him go.

"You've come up in the world, Chance," she said quietly.

Chance met her gaze for a moment, then smiled. "A bit."

"Do you need me to call you chief in public?" She was only half teasing. A lot had changed around here if wealthy ranchers were treating Chance Morgan like an equal. He'd obviously earned respect around Comfort Creek, and she'd have to catch up.

He laughed softly. "Only if you're going to boss around my officers."

She felt the heat rise in her cheeks. Her first instinct wasn't always the best choice...something that *hadn't* changed, apparently. "I am sorry about that."

"Forget it." He picked up his sandwich. "Weren't we going to talk business?"

Sadie nodded, took another spoonful of soup, then wiped her lips with a napkin.

"I had an idea for the ceremony, actually," she said. "I know you aren't crazy about this ceremony at all, but if you'd just hear me out on this one..."

"Shoot." He took a bite of his sandwich.

"I was thinking we could have some simple write-ups about each of the young men," Sadie said. "While those introductions to the men are being read, I'd like to have each man's favorite song being played in the background—an introduction to him as a person, not just as a serviceman. I'd also like to have some pictures of family put up onto a large screen, too. Before they joined them military they were boys, teenagers—"

"No." Chance's expression hardened.

"It would be tasteful, Chance," she said.

"I know you don't want things to get over-done, but—"

"I said *no*."

She'd expected this reaction, considering what he'd said during their last meeting, but it was a little too late to take this back. She'd already pitched the idea to the mayor, who loved it. It was now up to her to get Chance onboard.

"I think it would be fitting to show these men as more than their careers, though," she said. "They were certainly more than that to Comfort Creek."

They were moving away from their earlier comfortable dynamic, and Chance's posture was straightening, growing more rigid. He put down the sandwich and wiped his fingers on a napkin.

"I told you before," Chance replied, his voice controlled and low. "My brother's personal photos—his memory—are not for public consumption."

"He deserves to be remembered, though," she countered.

"And he *is* remembered." Chance shot her an irritated look. "If he turns into some sentimentalized meme article online, it isn't his memory that will be passed around, it'll be something else... I don't even know what. I don't want my brother's personal history being used for someone else's agenda."

"What if we banned cameras?" she suggested.

"Have you asked the mayor about that?"

She frowned. "No."

"He won't go for it," Chance said. "The mayor has his own agenda, too."

"Is this because of me, Chance?" she asked. "If the mayor had hired another event coordinator—"

"No, it isn't personal, Sadie. This has *nothing* to do with you."

His word choice stung. *Nothing*. She didn't have a right to grieve for the man she'd walked out on, but she didn't believe him, either, that he wasn't being just a little more difficult than he would have been with just about anybody else.

"What if I could guarantee that there would be no cameras present, and the ceremony wouldn't be recorded in any way?" she said. "Would that make a difference for you?"

Chance sighed and looked away. It wouldn't make any difference—she could tell. Why was he digging in like this? The town wanted to honor his brother, nothing more. Noah had been loved, as had the other young men, and

Comfort Creek wasn't taking their sacrifices for granted. That should matter.

"Sadie, can we just have a dignified military ceremony, please?" he asked quietly. "Leave the personal stuff out of it."

"Actually…" It was time to come clean. "Chance, I'm really sorry, but I already suggested the personal slant to the mayor."

"And he loved the idea," Chance concluded woodenly.

"He did."

Chance closed his eyes for a couple of beats, and she could see the exhaustion written all over his face. He opened his eyes again and fixed her with an unreadable look.

"The mayor thought it would honor our heroes," she said when he'd been silent for a moment or two. "The intention is positive."

"Yeah," Chance said. "Got it."

"Chance, why?" She leaned forward, catching his eye and holding it. "Why is this so hard for you?"

Chance heaved a sigh. "Because I don't like to do my grieving in public, Sadie. As police chief, I have a very public job, but that doesn't mean I'm the kind of guy who likes to share the most personal parts of myself with the

whole town. My twin brother—his death—
that's one of the private things."

He'd always been a private man. Even when
she'd been dating Noah, she used to enjoy trying to pull Chance out of his shell. He didn't
give up his thoughts or feelings easily. He hid
them behind that professional mask of his, and
it was easy to forget that it was just that—a
mask. There were real feelings under there.

"If I'd known…" She *should have* known…
she could see that now. She'd been gone for
five years, and she'd forgotten too much.

"You might have if you'd bothered coming
back before now."

"Well, I'm back now," she said. What else
could she do?

"Just in time to put together a commemorative ceremony for the family you didn't want to
be a part of." His expression was grim. "Look,
Sadie, I don't mean to be a jerk, but you're not
the right person to be planning this ceremony."

"Maybe not," she said curtly. "But I'm the
one the mayor hired."

He nodded. "True."

"So where does this leave us?" she asked.

"Nothing's changed," he replied with a
shake of his head. "We have to work together,

but first, I'm going to talk to the mayor myself. That personal slant has to go."

That was fair enough. She didn't really care if the ceremony had a personal element or not. What she cared about was honoring the fallen men and making sure Mayor Scott was happy with her work. Her guilt and her tangled feelings when it came to Chance Morgan would all have to wait until she could sort them out privately. She had to keep her head clear and do her job.

Chapter Five

Chance waited until after dinner before he drove toward the mayor's house on an acreage outside of town. The sun was slipping down below the horizon, dappling the sky with pink and orange that spilled over the snow-laden fields. He liked this time of day—when it felt like the sunset was painted just for him.

Lord, I wasn't ready for her...

That was the problem with all of this. He could have handled the mayor on his own, but with Sadie in the mix, everything felt out of control. And it didn't help that with her back in town, he was dealing with all sorts of emotions he thought he'd safely sealed away—anger at the woman who broke his brother's heart, guilt over his role in her escape, grief over his brother's death and most uncomfortable of all was that empty hollow loneliness that had been left behind when Sadie left town. No goodbye. No warning. At the very least she could have explained herself. But nothing. She'd just left. And he couldn't tell anyone—especially not his brother—what that did to him.

He'd felt incredibly guilty as he helped his brother empty Sadie's things out of his home, because while he was comforting Noah, he felt that hole she'd left behind, too. And after he'd gone back to his own house again, he'd sat there alone, feeling that ache deep in his chest. He wasn't supposed to feel this way. He was supposed to be angry on his brother's behalf. He knew what he was *supposed* to be, but that didn't change facts.

Well, now Sadie was back, and her presence made everything more difficult. She shouldn't be the one in charge of anything to honor Noah, but she was. And she had the mayor wrapped around her finger. Sadie was still just as pretty and full of life as she'd always been, and somehow that seemed wrong. Noah was dead, and because of that, everyone else had changed—why not her?

He remembered driving Sadie out to the mayor's house a few months before the wedding. Noah had been doing a framing job on a guest cottage on the mayor's land, and Chance had been bringing Sadie out to see her fiancé. It was spring but not exactly warm, and he remembered how she'd been dressed—jeans, pink rubber boots, a fleecy sweater and these white, fuzzy mittens.

You look ridiculous, he'd teased her. *Lose the mittens.*

I'm weather appropriate, she'd countered. *Who cares how I look?*

Truthfully, she'd been beautiful—always had been. He just hated admitting that, because she wasn't his to admire.

True, he'd agreed. *You sure Noah wants to be bugged at work?*

I'm delivering his birthday gift. She'd pulled a small package out of her pocket mysteriously. *He won't mind being disturbed for presents.*

What did you get him?

It's a surprise.

I won't tease you, promise. He'd honestly been curious at that point.

It's hard to tell if you're serious or not. She'd squinted at him with mock solemnity. *You could be arresting me or wishing me a happy birthday, and I doubt your expression would change.*

That day as he drove her out toward Noah's work site at the mayor's house, Chance could still remember that overwhelming surge of regret he'd felt as he drove his brother's fiancée out to see him…because after Noah had been dating Sadie for a few years, Chance was supposed to be over his feelings for her. So he pretended not to feel anything more than brotherly concern, but his professional reserve covered things he didn't dare reveal.

That was a lifetime ago now. Noah was gone, and none of those old competitions mattered anymore. But Sadie was back. Sadie was not only his brother's ex, but she was the one who'd pushed Noah to the edge. If it hadn't been for Sadie's callous rejection, Noah would still be taking on carpentry jobs around Comfort Creek. Noah had turned to the army out of heartbreak…and Chance was to blame, too. He'd been hiding his feelings for years, and he should have stayed away. Going to her house the night before the wedding had been reckless. He should have known that something would slip.

Mayor Scott lived on the top of a hill in a large ranch-style house with a four-car garage and a flagpole out front. Chance turned into the long drive and swerved around a pothole. As he pulled up in front of the garage, he glanced over at the flag. It was at half-mast.

Still. It had been at half-mast for two years, ever since Ryan was killed.

The sun had set by the time Chance got out of his cruiser and headed toward the house. The lights were on inside—all of them, by the looks of it. The house positively glowed, but when he knocked at the front door, there was no response.

Chance glanced at his watch, then knocked again, this time harder. A couple of minutes later, the door opened and he was met with Susan Scott, the mayor's wife. Her hair was cut short, but not styled in any particular way. Just short and blunt. Gray. She wore some makeup, but it didn't do much for her—not lately. She used to be a woman who glowed with joy, but her smile looked almost painful now.

"Oh, hello, Chief." She stepped back, her slippered feet swishing against the hardwood floor. "Come in. My husband is…" She looked behind her as if expecting to see him, then turned back and sighed. "Come in."

Chance wiped his feet on the rug and followed her through the entryway, past the kitchen and down a hallway. The sound of a television newscast came from behind a closed door, and she tapped on it.

"Susie?" It was the mayor's voice, and the TV suddenly silenced. "Come in, sweetheart."

She opened the door and stepped back. Mayor Scott sat in an armchair facing a now blackened TV screen. He wore slippers, too, and he looked older in that position. When he spotted Chance, he pushed down the footrest and clumsily rose to his feet.

"Chief! Good to see you." The smile changed—he was professional again, and Chance momentarily regretted bothering the mayor at home, but he figured that they might be able to talk a little more openly this way.

"Sorry to intrude, sir," Chance said. "I was hoping to talk to you."

"Of course, of course. Susan—" But when the mayor turned to the doorway, it was empty. His wife had already retreated. The mayor's smile faltered again, and he shut the door behind Chance. "She's not doing so well."

"Is she sick?" Chance asked.

"No, just losing Ryan… She's not the woman she used to be."

Chance could see that clearly.

"She can't handle the news anymore," the mayor said, leaning against the edge of his desk and indicating a wooden visitor's chair for Chance. "I watch it with the door shut so she won't hear anything that will upset her. She's very fragile lately."

Chance nodded, but he remained standing. "I can see that."

"Anyway." The mayor fixed Chance with a questioning look. "What can I do for you?"

Chance glanced behind the mayor, out the window to the backyard. He could see the guest cottage his brother had framed in the light from the window. It was the one part of this home that wasn't aglow.

"I had a meeting with Miss Jenkins today," Chance said. "And she told me about her ideas for a personal ceremony."

"Yes. Brilliant." Mayor Scott nodded. "She's very good at this, you know. I knew that if you two just sat down together—"

"I hate it." He hadn't meant to come out with it quite that way, but the words were honest.

The mayor raised his eyebrows. "Have you heard her out?"

"Sir, Sadie Jenkins walked out on my brother. She didn't want him, broke his heart and humiliated him in front of the entire town. She doesn't deserve to be the one to plan a ceremony in honor of the man she cast aside."

"It is also in honor of Ryan, and of Michael

Flores and Terrance West," the mayor pointed out. "And she's very talented."

"Anyone else, sir," Chance said. "Please."

"Do you think we're awash in event planners out here in Comfort Creek?" the mayor asked with a low laugh. "I didn't exactly have a long list of applicants."

"Maybe between you and I—"

"Chance..." the mayor said. "Susan really likes her."

Chance glanced toward the closed door out of instinct, then back at the mayor. "Mrs. Scott likes her? With all due respect, sir, I don't see how that factors in right now."

"You aren't a married man," Mayor Scott replied with a small smile. "I know you think that I'm just some selfish old fool who wants a ceremony his own way. But it's not for me, Chance. It's for her."

Chance didn't want a ceremony, period, but if he had to compromise, he could help to put together something appropriate and imper-sonal.

"Sir, we could still have the ceremony, but—"

"That woman lost her son." The older man pointed toward the door and his finger trem-bled. "She lost him two years ago, and the light went out inside of her. She can't let go, she can't cry. She just crumbles a little more every day. And when I said we'd honor the boys—do it up right—she liked that, and it brought her back just a little bit. But she didn't want it to be some cold military event, she wanted it to honor *her boy*. Can you understand that?"

"Yes, sir, I can..."

The thing that would comfort Susan Scott most was the thing that would be of least comfort to Chance and his parents. His mom and dad were the private type, too—just wanting to deal with their loss as a family. But they weren't crumbling, and Susan was.

"So I'm asking you to work with Sadie on a ceremony for Susan," the mayor said. "We all grieve differently, son, and she needs our help right now. So work with Sadie—she knows what I'm wanting, and maybe now you can see why."

Chance sighed and glanced out the window at that guest cottage once more. Everything that Noah had built was still there...but it felt different. Susan needed this, and that did change things.

"Yeah. I'll—" He sucked in a breath. "I'll see what we can do."

"Thank you." The mayor nodded. "It's appreciated."

"Sorry for the intrusion, sir," Chance said. "I'll see myself out."

Chance met Susan in the hallway, she saw him to the door. She gave him a smile that didn't reach her eyes.

"Nice to see you again, Chief," she said. "How are you keeping?"

"I'm alright," he said with a smile. "And you?"

She crossed her arms over her stomach. "This time of year…it's the hardest for me. It was in January that Ryan died."

"Hang in there, Mrs. Scott," Chance said quietly. "It gets better."

She didn't answer him, and he didn't press her. Chance opened the door and stepped outside into the crisp winter air. He heard the door shut behind him as he headed toward his cruiser. All of this would be so much easier if it were just about an egotistical mayor and his desire to control the whole event.

Maybe Chance would have to be more flexible, after all. He hated to admit to Sadie being right about something, but she'd said that he wasn't the only one who was grieving, and he obviously wasn't. They'd have to find a way to make the ceremony a healing experience for everyone.

Maybe even for him, too.

* * *

The next day, Sadie pushed her cart across the snowy parking lot of Comfort Creek's grocery store. Her car wasn't far away, but the snow made the small cart wheels stick, so she had to throw her weight behind it, everything in the cart jiggling so much that she was worried about the eggs. The day was overcast and a cold wind whipped her hair into her face and then back again, leaving a few strands stuck to her lip gloss. It was one of those days where she wished she could go back to bed.

"Sadie Jenkins?"

Sadie looked toward the voice and spotted her old friend Harper Kemp. She stood on the sidewalk next to the parking lot, shading her eyes with one gloved hand. Her fiery curls poked out from under a snug cloche hat. They'd been best friends, but that had changed.

Sadie inwardly grimaced. She hadn't seen Harper since the wedding. Harper had been her maid of honor, and she'd been waiting at the church with everyone else when Sadie changed her mind. Sadie had sent her a few emails after she'd left, but there was a chill between them ever since Sadie's disappearing act, and she couldn't even blame her. Harper was about three years younger than she was, and while the difference in their ages hadn't seemed to matter in their friendship, it might have started to matter a little more when it came down to life experience. Harper just couldn't understand.

"Harper!" Sadie forced a smile. She'd have to do this sooner or later.

"I'd heard you were back in town," the younger woman said, stepping over the curb and heading in Sadie's direction. "I'd hoped you'd call."

Seriously? So had five years been enough for Harper to forgive her? That would be a nice change of pace. Sadie stopped at her car and popped the trunk to load the groceries.

"Sorry," Sadie said, lifting the first bag into her trunk. "I've been working since pretty much as soon as I got back, so I haven't had the chance to touch base. How are you doing?" Sadie leaned over and gave her friend a hug. "How's the store?"

Harper's family ran Blessings Bridal, the only bridal shop until Fort Collins, which was sixty miles east. Sadie had spent hours in that store, searching for the right gown with Harper...as much as that was worth now. Sadie now owned a boxed wedding dress that she'd worn for all of an hour while talking herself out of her own wedding.

"Everything's great." Harper smiled and pushed her red curls away from her eyes. "I'm managing the store now and Dad has fully retired."

Sadie shot her friend a smile. "That's good news."

"Yep." Harper nodded, and there was a beat of silence.

"Are you free for a coffee right now?" Sadie asked, and as soon as the words were out of her mouth, she regretted them. She wasn't sure how much more rejection she could handle, and she was almost certain that Harper would turn her down.

Harper glanced at her watch. "Sure. I could make the time."

Sadie smiled. That was unexpected, and coffee with a friend would be nice right about now. She loaded the last of her groceries into the trunk, looked down Main Street toward the coffee shop. It wasn't far.

"I'm sorry I didn't try more," Harper said as they walked down the sidewalk together. "I should have put a little more effort into keeping in touch."

"It's okay." Sadie pushed her gloved hands

into the pockets of her red, woolen coat. It had hurt a lot when Harper hadn't been more supportive, but she understood it. She'd hurt a good man, and a lot of people would probably think she should have just gone through and married him at that point.

"I didn't understand then," Harper went on. "I do now, though."

"You do?" Sadie looked over cautiously.

"My brother got divorced last year," Harper said. The news took Sadie by surprise. Martin's wedding had been the talk of the town for years after the event.

"Martin's divorced?" Sadie shook her head.

They'd brought in a horse-drawn carriage, and Martin's wife, Laney, was dressed in a princess-style ball gown. It was all so over-the-top compared to Comfort Creek's usual fare that there were people who'd kept their *bonbonnières* from the day and still brought them out for conversation. She was surprised her grandmother hadn't told her about this.

"What happened?" Sadie asked.

"Martin said she kept pulling her parents into all their arguments," Harper said. "And then there was the debt from the wedding. Martin wanted to pay it off as fast as possible and Laney wanted the big house right away.

Her parents wanted to give them a down payment for the house, but Martin didn't want to take it. It was just stress on top of stress."

Laney had wanted all the things that Noah had offered Sadie...the wedding, the house, the stability. She could see the irony there. Some women wanted exactly that—so badly, that they'd ruined their marriages over it, apparently. Sadie had been willing to walk away from all of it in order to avoid marrying the wrong man. But that's what Harper thought Sadie would be like as a married woman? It wasn't a flattering view.

"And this makes you understand me how?" Sadie asked cautiously. She wasn't even sure she wanted an honest answer to that. But then, she hadn't stayed to defend herself, so maybe she shouldn't be too offended.

"The divorce was awful. Bitter, painful. They went at each other's throats," Harper said. "It was worse than a canceled wedding, I can tell you that. I can see why you decided to end it sooner rather than later. I should have been more supportive of that."

She felt a surge of relief. Harper was the first person besides Nana to say that.

"Thank you." Sadie blinked back an unexpected mist of tears. "I'm sorry for Martin. And Laney, too, for that matter."

"Me, too." Harper smiled wanly.

"Chance doesn't see it your way, though," Sadie added as they took a long step over a slushy puddle.

"What do you mean?" Harper asked, stopping at the door to the coffee shop.

"He's furious I left. Period." Sadie shook her head. "And no amount of logic seems to change that."

It was personal for Chance. She'd left all of them in his eyes—at least that's how it seemed to Sadie. He also thought she'd pushed Noah into the army. And maybe she had…that was the worst part. She'd blamed herself for breaking his heart, for walking away, for not seeing that their relationship wouldn't work sooner. She'd blamed herself for an awful lot, but until she'd gotten back here, she'd never seen any reason to blame herself for her ex-fiancé's death.

They opened the door and headed into the coffee-scented warmth. The women stamped the snow from their boots and Sadie unwound her scarf from her neck.

"Everyone grieves differently, I suppose,"

Harper said, but she cast Sadie a sympathetic glance.

They placed their orders for two large coffees with cream, then headed for a table in a far corner that seemed relatively private. The table overlooked the snowy street, and Sadie remembered that the last time she'd been in this shop, she'd been butting heads with Chance over the ceremony plans.

"Chance took it really hard when you left," Harper said.

"He was mad, I know that," Sadie agreed.

"No, I mean—" Harper sighed. "Noah had to clean out all your stuff from the house. So I came by with my dad's truck to pick it up and bring it to your grandmother's place. You know, the kitchen stuff you were moving in, that dresser that you'd refinished…"

Sadie nodded. She'd been trying to put her mark on that house, but no matter what she brought into it, it still hadn't felt like home.

"So while they were loading up the truck, Noah threw a key chain into a box, and Chance pulled it out again. He told Noah that one day he'd want to remember you."

A lump rose in Sadie's throat. It was hard to listen to this—to hear about how Noah had swept his home clean of her. She and Noah had shared lots of happy memories in that house, including barbecues they'd hosted and getting it ready for her to move in after the wedding. They'd been happy together—happy enough, at least. And while she could understand Noah needing to purge himself of memories in order to heal...

"I'm sorry," Harper said with a wince. "The point of the story was that Chance hadn't wanted to just wipe you out of their memories. He wanted them to remember you."

"What did the key chain look like?" she asked numbly.

"It was metal. Engraved. I didn't get a really close look. Chance pocketed it."

He'd kept it anyway? Sadie sighed. She'd given Noah that key chain on his birthday just before their wedding. She'd gotten Chance to give her a ride out to where Noah was working so that she could surprise him. She remembered how she used to chip away at his reserved personality, and she knew she could take liberties with that serious cop that no one else could because she was special to him. Like a little sister. But after that moment on the porch when they'd almost kissed, she would never have been able to see him as just a brother again.

"I missed him, you know," Sadie said softly.

"Of course you would," Harper replied. "You almost married him."

But she wasn't talking about Noah. She meant Chance. She'd grieved her relationship with Noah, and then she'd grieved his death when she learned of it, but somehow, she hadn't been able to grieve for the rest of it—for the friendship she'd had with her soon-to-be brother-in-law, for example. She hadn't expected to miss Chance like that, either. But he'd given her more than she'd realized—propped up the relationship with her brother that hadn't ever been enough to really fulfill her. Noah and his family were an attractive package, but she knew it was wrong to rely on all of them like that. Noah should have been enough on his own, and if she'd needed Chance in the picture to make her marriage to his brother work, well, that was just wrong, and she recognized that.

"Well…" Sadie pulled herself together. "It was a long time ago. I'm actually starting up an event planning business here in town."

Harper's eyebrows rose in interest. "I'd heard that. So you settled on something, then?"

"What can I say? I finally found something I liked enough to stick with."

"So what's your plan?"

The rest of the conversation revolved around both women's businesses. When she'd lived in Comfort Creek before, she'd worked various jobs—a night clerk at the hotel along the highway, a baking assistant at the bakery, an activities coordinator for a nursing home. But now that she was back in town, she was proud to be building a career that relied upon her creative strengths. She was in her early thirties now, and she wasn't just a woman with a job, she was a woman building a business—she liked that distinction.

She needed to make her life here about something else—not her history with the town's chief of police.

Chapter Six

When Chance and Noah were teenagers, they'd competed fiercely about everything from grades to backyard football matches. That changed when they reached adulthood and started following their own career paths, but there had always been a tinge of competition between them even as men. Thanksgiving was never complete without a little touch football…which quickly turned into full contact. They both enjoyed lifting weights to keep in shape, and they'd text each other with joking trash talk. In fact, his brother's text was often the spur Chance needed to get himself out the door and to the gym on a frigid winter morning. If he missed a workout, he'd never hear the end of it. *Slept late, huh? Meeting the girls for brunch, or something?*

There were a couple of women on the force

who could flatten Noah for talk like that, and then go to brunch afterward. But that had been their brotherly dynamic. It didn't help that they had similar taste in women, either. When it came to Sadie, Chance might have tried to turn her attention, except that he saw something different in the way Noah looked at her. His brother was smitten, and competition was one thing, but when it came down to the stuff that mattered, he had his brother's back. And Sadie mattered to Noah.

Chance sat in his office. The snow drifted down in windy swirls outside the small window. Ice had crept along the bottom of the inside of the glass, a frosty layer that wouldn't go away until spring. Across from him sat Toby Gillespie.

"So how are you finding patrol in Comfort Creek?" Chance asked, pulling his mind back to the job at hand.

"Honestly, sir, it's a little dull," Toby replied. "There have been a few disputes between neighbors, but other than that, it's dead calm."

Chance nodded. "That's the way we like to keep it. Lots of time to think."

Toby didn't answer that one, but Comfort Creek was perfect for this program for exactly that reason. They weren't here for teaching tactical defense strategies, they were here for the stuff that lay at the bottom of these officers—the sediment of experience and emotion that had settled long, long ago. Without some calm and some quiet, they'd never get deep enough to ever reach it.

"So today, I want you to interview me," Chance said.

"I've been thinking about that, sir," Toby said. "Why don't we just have the families fill out a form or something?"

"Because forms are cold and distant," Chance said with a wry smile.

"They could be…warmly written."

Chance chuckled. "About as warm and inviting as those binders in the basement."

His warning was taken to heart, because Toby smiled, ever so slightly. "Fine. So what information am I supposed to get from you?"

Chance slid a paper across his desk toward his trainee. "It's all on there. So let's start."

Toby scanned the page, his posture straightening, his expression granite. He pulled a pen out of his pocket and gave it a click. "Okay. So let's start with the name of the deceased."

They obviously had a lot of work to do. Toby's manner was definitely removed, which could be appropriate in some police interviews—just not this kind.

"The name of my brother," Chance corrected him. "Besides, you don't really need to clarify that information. You have his name. Maybe we should ease into this a little bit. You're talking to someone who lost his twin brother a year ago. We were close, he and I. It's better to find out what relationship that person had to the man who died."

"Right." Toby cleared his throat. "So I should start with, 'Are you a family member of—'" he looked down at his page "'—Noah Emerson Morgan?'"

"I am." Chance nodded. "I was. He was my brother."

"What branch of military was your brother in?"

"Army."

"What was his rank?" Toby asked.

"Lieutenant. He wanted to become an officer, and he would have, if he'd lived."

Toby nodded and made a note. He paused. "I was an officer."

"Yeah?" Chance leaned back in his chair. He knew all of this, but he wanted to hear it from Toby. "How many men did you lead?"

"Thirty. Twenty-four came back." Toby's

gaze flickered up, then down to his page again. "I haven't forgotten their faces. I owe it to them."

"That's a heavy burden," Chase said quietly.

Toby sighed. "I know I made the right calls. I know that. I got twenty-four back alive, and if I'd made different choices, we might have all died out there. But the ones you lose hang on you. Which is why I didn't want to do this—contact families."

"Do you think they'll blame you?" Chance asked.

"I blame me." Toby tapped the page. He was silent for a couple of beats, then took a breath. "Okay, so did your brother die in action?"

"Friendly fire during a practice exercise in Afghanistan."

"I think I heard about that." Toby looked up, and for the first time Chance saw sympathy in his eyes. "Pointless."

"Yeah." That was exactly how Chance felt about it, too. It wasn't a sacrifice for his country. No ground was gained.

"So…" Toby turned back to the sheet. "Did he earn any medals? Any honors?"

They went through the rest of the questions, and when they were finished, Toby's granite mask had slipped away, and in its place was a tired, sad man.

"I'm not sure I'm the one to do this job, sir," Toby said.

"I disagree," Chance said. "You understand what these men went through. That matters to a family."

"Every single one of those men, your brother included, had a commanding officer," Toby said.

"Every officer has split-second decisions to make," Chance agreed. "So does every cop. You go with your training—and I know you've been following protocol to a T. But when your life isn't on the line, it's okay to let them know that you're human."

"*Weak*, you mean," Toby said wryly.

"I stand by *human*." Chance slid another page across his desk. "These are the families of the other men who died over the last five years. Start by finding out their personal relationship to the man and take it from there."

Toby didn't touch the page for a moment, then reached out and put his hand over it. "I'm sorry about your brother, sir."

"Thank you." Chance felt a lump rise in his throat. "He was a good guy."

Toby rose to his feet. "Permission to be dismissed, sir?"

"Granted."

Toby met Chance's gaze for a split second, then saluted and turned toward the door. Six men. That was why Toby hid behind the rules and regulations. He'd lost six men and he couldn't live with himself if he made another mistake. Mistakes in the army were deadly. Mistakes in the police force could be deadly, too, but not as often. And not normally in Comfort Creek.

Chance sat there in the quiet for a long time. He knew what it felt like to be responsible for a death, because he'd been part of the pressure that drove his brother away. When they'd cleaned Sadie's stuff out of Noah's house, Toby had thrown an engraved key chain into a box, and Chance had retrieved it.

He told himself it was because his brother needed to hold on to something from his time with Sadie…but that hadn't been true. It had been for him. *He* hadn't wanted to let her go entirely yet. *He* wasn't ready for her leaving to be final.

Chance had been in love with his brother's fiancée, and he'd made his peace with that. Sadie was the whole package—beautiful, funny, sweet and definitely hard to get. And he hadn't been able to shake free of his feelings for her. So he told his brother that he'd want to remember her. Maybe not today or tomorrow, but eventually. She did represent five years of his brother's life. So he'd kept that key chain and he'd put it into his pocket while he watched Harper Kemp drive off with a truckload of personal effects to be delivered to Abigail Jenkins.

Let me see that. Noah had held out his hand, and Chance handed it over. Noah looked at it morosely for a few beats, then nodded slowly. *You're right. I can't just wipe out five years, can I?*

When Noah got back from his first deployment, Chance saw his brother fiddling with that same engraved key chain. It was scratched up, but he still recognized it. His brother had taken it with him—a touchstone from home. It had been in his pocket on the day he was shot.

And Chance couldn't help but wonder—if he hadn't snatched up that key chain…if he hadn't been trying to hold on to Sadie in some small part of his own heart, would things have been different? So maybe Noah wouldn't have been able to erase five years of his own life, but would it have killed Chance to just let his brother believe he could for a little while? And if he'd done that, would Noah have been able to deal with his heartbreak in his own way, and maybe have stayed home to do it?

Sometimes, it was the smallest things that proved to be pivotal in a life—a sermon, a piece of advice, a fragment of a song. For them, that pivotal moment wasn't so innocuous—it was a betrayal. Chance had almost kissed Sadie and then burdened her with his feelings for her. His brother never knew, but it had all started to topple with Chance's moment of weakness.

Noah had tried to sweep himself clean of Sadie. He'd *tried*. Chance should have left well enough alone. He'd shouldered these feelings for her for years already, and he could have done it for a little longer.

That evening, Sadie stood in the aisle at Comfort Creek's Craft Corner, the only crafting shop they had. It was well stocked, though, and Sadie was perusing some dollhouse items. There was a tiny kitchen stove that could be lit using a tea light. It was actually functional, and while the idea of being able to cook tiny meals on doll dishes was entrancing, she wasn't really about to do it. Still, it was hard to turn away.

"I just got those in," Liz, the store owner, said from where she sat on her haunches, dusting a shelf. "There are all sorts of YouTube videos with tiny cooking. Ridiculously soothing. Have you seen them?"

"No." Sadie chuckled. "But Nana probably has."

Gone were the days of Nana needing help with her Wi-Fi, apparently. Sadie moved down the aisle, scanning items they didn't need. She was tempted to start a new dollhouse—a neighbor for the existing house. She wouldn't, though. Her eye fell on a tiny mop and bucket, and she grinned. It would be perfect for the corner of the kitchen.

"I think I'll get this, Liz," she said.

Liz pushed herself to her feet and headed to the cash register with Sadie.

"Your grandmother's dollhouse is just amazing. She could make a fortune off of it, you know," Liz said as she rang up the sale. "There are people eager to buy a completely furnished dollhouse, and they'll pay a pretty penny for it, too."

"Sell it?" The thought was almost painful. That dollhouse was more than a collector's item, it was the best part of her childhood. "Never. My grandmother just made hand-stitched quilts for the beds."

"I know." Liz put a hand over her heart. "It's

stunning. The time and effort that goes into something like that... You're right. It's about more than money."

Sadie paid and took her change. She'd been here looking at the dollhouse items, but she'd also been looking at different options to decorate the town square for the upcoming ceremony. There were a few things she liked, but she hadn't made a final decision yet.

"How long will it take to order in those streamers?" Sadie asked.

"For an extra fee I can have them rushed overnight," Liz replied. "Just let me know when you decide, and I'll put in the order."

"Thanks, Liz. I appreciate it. I'll be in touch."

Liz picked up her dusting rag again and waved as Sadie headed toward the door. Outside, the sun had set and the streetlights left golden pools on the snowbanks. She paused to wrap her scarf around her neck and pull on her gloves before she pushed open the door and stepped out into the winter night.

She'd walked to the store this evening because she wanted the fresh air and some time to think. It had been great to reconnect with Harper, and it brought back a flood of memories of when she thought this town and a loving husband would be enough for her. It was ironic that she was back, still believing this town could be enough. It hadn't been before…

But Comfort Creek hadn't been the problem, it was her. She could still remember the flood of relief as she stepped on the gas and headed out of town toward the open highway. Maybe that was how her mother had felt, too, when she'd driven off with her musician boyfriend, leaving Comfort Creek and the pressures of motherhood behind her. Lori had always been holding out for something better on the horizon, and as much as Sadie resented her mother for that instability, she'd ended up just like her.

Sadie angled her steps toward home, and in some ways, it was as if those five years away from this town just evaporated. Comfort Creek was no different—the craft shop, the town hall, the muffled silence of snowy streets… Her feet knew the way home without her even having to think about it, and she smiled to herself, thinking about giving Nana the tiny mop. She'd love it. Nana was the easiest person to buy gifts for—something for the dollhouse never disappointed.

The sidewalk ended and Sadie stepped off the curb to continue up the road when her boot hit a patch of ice hidden under the snowfall.

Her heart leaped to her throat, and if a panicked gasp aimed heavenward could count as a prayer—

Her leg twisted under her and she went down heavily, her breath knocked out of her lungs. She sat there for a moment, catching her breath. Her knee ached from the way she'd twisted it and her hip was sore both from landing and the cold from the snow, but that was the worst of it.

"Ouch…" She eased forward to get up just as she heard the rumble of a motor behind her on the road. She turned to see a police cruiser. Comfort Creek was the best-patrolled town in America with all these sensitivity trainees driving around, and tonight she was grateful for that. The car pulled to a stop and she saw Chance in the driver's seat, concern written all over his face. He pushed open the door and left it open as he tramped through the snow and bent down to help her up.

"You okay?" He offered her his hand and she took it, then winced as she rose to her feet. Her backside was covered in snow and her leg hurt. She bent to rub her knee.

"Fine." She laughed self-consciously. "I just slipped on some ice. Thanks."

Chance didn't let go of her right away, keeping a hold of her arm as she wiped herself off with the other hand. She felt embarrassed by the fall, and also a little shaken. She was grudgingly glad to have Chance there to help her back up. She pulled the little bag out of her pocket and was disappointed to see that the tiny mop handle had been snapped when she landed on it.

"I'm fine," she repeated, and he let go of her.

Chance didn't move, however, and when she looked up, she caught a flicker of the old Chance in his expression, and she felt a wave of such nostalgia that it almost brought tears to her eyes.

"That must have hurt," Chance said, misreading her expression. "You want a ride home?"

"Sure." It wasn't far, but between the cold and her sore knee, it wouldn't be a comfortable walk. "Thanks, Chance."

It felt like old times—back when she had Chance and Noah looking out for her…back when she was on the verge of becoming a Morgan, too. It had been safe and comforting in a way she hadn't fully appreciated back then.

Chance opened the passenger-side door and Sadie limped over and eased into the warm seat. Chance got back into the driver's side.

He put the car into gear and pulled away from the curb. She stole a glance at him from the corner of her eye.

"Thanks for stopping," she said.

"Part of the job." But there was a slight up-turn to his lips as he said it. He was softening up a bit—she could feel it.

"I ran into Harper today," she said.

"Yeah? How's she doing?"

"Good." Sadie rubbed at her knee again. "She told me about Martin and Laney. The divorce and all that."

"Oh, yeah." The snow crunched under the tires as they eased up the street. "That was pretty bad. Didn't your grandmother fill you in?"

"Not much." She leaned back. Maybe Nana thought it was too sordid, or perhaps there were bigger things happening with Sadie's mother at the time to monopolize their conversation. "Chance, that could have been me and Noah."

"Bitterly divorced?" he asked, and she couldn't tell by his tone what he was feeling.

"Noah was a good man—more than good. Everyone knows that. Noah was a catch, but he wasn't right for me. And I wasn't right for him."

"Could have fooled me," he said, his tone low. "He really loved you."

"I know." She sighed. "But it's possible to really love someone who isn't good for you."

Loving Sadie hadn't been good for Noah. Some people were like that—and it looked like she'd inherited that trait from her mom.

"He'd have been loyal," Chance said. "He'd have been honest and a hard worker. You'd never have wanted for anything."

Sadie knew all that—that was exactly why it had taken her so long to walk away from him. Noah had been a great guy, and he'd loved her. She knew that didn't come along every day, but she still believed she couldn't have been happy with him—not completely.

"It wasn't the money, Chance." She heard the resentment in her own voice.

"I'm not saying—" he started.

"I didn't want to get married in order to have financial security." She pulled off her gloves. "Marriage should be more than that. I wanted to marry a man who, when you took away the money and the career, stripped away the family—if it was just he and I, no one else—I'd be willing to live with in poverty by ourselves, if that's what it came to."

"Stripping away the family?" Chance shot her an unfathomable look.

"I don't mean that I'd ever want to get rid of a man's family," she clarified. "But with Noah and the rest of you—you were a package deal. And that was wonderful! I loved you guys. Your family was part of the draw with Noah, and that didn't seem right, somehow."

"It doesn't seem like such a bad thing from where I'm sitting," he retorted.

"If I wanted Noah so long as the rest of you were in the picture, what if something happened? I mean, what if Noah and I had to move far away and it was just the two of us? What if your parents decided to move to Florida to retire, and you got married and headed to Beverly Hills? What then? Would I still be happy with just Noah in Comfort Creek?"

"Beverly Hills, huh?"

"Then Cleveland. I don't care. You know what I'm getting at. It isn't right to marry a man for the good times, if I wouldn't be grateful to be by his side in the bad times."

"And me in Beverly Hills—that's the bad times?" She could hear the dry humor in his tone.

"Misery." She rolled her eyes. "Chance, right now I might be Public Enemy Number

One, but you and I *were* friends. Don't you remember that? I know it got…complicated at the end, but…we got along so well. And your mom is just amazing. I mean, at this point she probably can't stand me, either, but I loved learning her recipes and listening to her stories about when you and Noah were little. That was the best part of the holidays with your family. And…I shouldn't have been that content with hanging out with the rest of you. I should have been a little more eager to get time alone with Noah. Don't you think?"

"So you liked being with the family more than you liked being alone with my brother?"

"Sort of," she admitted. "It's just that…I think we were missing something that should have been there."

"It was there for him," he said, and his words hit her in the gut.

"Maybe," she agreed softly. "But if I was going to vow for better or for worse, I needed to make sure I meant that. Because life can be hard, and you can end up with 'for worse' in a heartbeat."

He didn't answer, and his expression stayed stoically immobile, just the way it always was. The house was coming up, and Sadie looked at the pink shutters, comfortingly pretty against the white of the snow. She was home, but home was more than one person, or a house, or even the culmination of childhood memories. It was something more, and she could feel an empty ache inside of her. Whatever it was, she was still looking for it.

Lord, she prayed. *Why can't I just be content?*

She fiddled with the broken mop as Chance pulled up in front of the house. He parked and then looked over at her.

"I'm sorry about that," Chance said, nodding at the broken item in her hands. "Maybe you can glue it or something."

"I'm hoping." She smiled wanly. "Nana's been doing more work on the dollhouse. I guess I just wanted to be part of that again."

Chance nodded. "Let me give you a hand getting inside."

She looked out the window to the slick of ice on Nana's driveway. She'd spread some salt, and there were some melted patches.

"You don't have to, Chase." She could pick her way to the door.

"Sure, I do." His expression was still granite, but there was a hint of warmth in his eyes. "Hold on. I'm coming around."

He got out of the car and slammed the door

shut behind him before he started around the front of the vehicle to her side. She sat in the warm silence, watching him. A gentleman to the last. She knew that he hadn't forgiven her, but it was the cop in him, and possibly the Christian, that kept him doing his duty despite his personal feelings.

He arrived at her door and she pushed it open. She just missed the days when his kindness wasn't duty, but then, that was selfish on her part, too, because he'd been hiding deeper feelings back then and his kindness had probably been painful in a whole different way. She'd left town because she couldn't marry Noah, knowing that his brother was the one who made it all worthwhile, and she didn't have the right to ask for anything from Chance now.

Chapter Seven

Sadie paused and looked toward the wide wooden porch on the front of her grandmother's home. The last time she and Chance stood on that porch, it had been the night before her wedding. She pushed back the memories. Friends. That was the goal here. Was that too much for her to ask? She had to coexist in this town with the Morgans, and she had to forge something new with Chance—something distinct from the complicated friendship they'd had before.

"Have you seen Nana's dollhouse?" Sadie asked as she hobbled up the walk. It was a distraction mostly. What would Chance care about a dollhouse?

"No," he replied. "But Noah mentioned it. Said it was pretty impressive."

They reached the walkway that led to the

front steps. Her knee was sore and cold, and she was grateful when they reached the stairs. Chance went with her to the porch, then released her arm and took a step back.

"Thank you," she said, and she could feel her cheeks heat. She looked toward the door.

"Not a problem. Glad you're okay."

"Do you want to come in?" she asked. She was almost certain he'd say no, but he'd gone through the trouble of getting her safely home, and it only seemed polite to offer. She was also eager to get away from this spot filled with uncomfortable memories.

"I wouldn't mind seeing the famous dollhouse," he said, and a smile tickled one corner of his lips. He looked like the old Chance standing there. He was relaxed and there was that glitter in his eyes that most people didn't notice, but she did. She always used to know when Chance was joking, and most people couldn't tell.

Sadie pulled out her key and unlocked the door. "I can give you the tour."

Chance followed her into the warm house. It smelled of freshly baked cookies, and Nana looked up from an armchair where she was crocheting.

"I was going to show Chance the dollhouse," Sadie said.

"Of course." Nana put aside her doily and rose to her feet. "Hello, Chance. Nice to see you again. I just made a batch of cookies. I'll go rummage some up."

They bent to take off their boots, and Sadie took a little longer than Chance, easing the boot off her tender leg, then hung their coats on the hooks. Sadie led the way, limping slightly, down the hallway to the study. She turned on the light and stepped inside. The room was colder than the rest of the house, as usual, and she shivered. Chance filled the doorway, and when she glanced back at him, she caught his gaze fixed on her, not on the dollhouse. His attention flicked to the dollhouse when she'd noticed his scrutiny, but her cheeks still warmed. Was he remembering it, too—the last time he'd been here?

"It's amazing." Chance bent to look into the miniature rooms. "Wow—you two did this together?"

"Most of it." Sadie stepped closer and reached into the tiny kitchen to open a cupboard door. Inside was a miniature pitcher.

"This is really something." She could hear the smile in his voice.

"It helped—after Mom left," she admitted. "Gave me something else to focus on. My grandmother and I built our relationship as we put together this dollhouse. Nana had only started on it when I arrived. I guess I was pretty goal-oriented, even then."

"You always were…" he murmured.

"Did I tell you about my mother?" she asked.

"Not a lot."

"She wasn't satisfied. Ever. I remember her dating a guy who was really nice. I called him Uncle, and he visited a lot. He was sweet to both of us. She dumped him. She was always the one to do the dumping."

"Why did she dump him?"

"He wasn't right." Sadie shrugged. "I don't know. I was a kid. I didn't really understand the relationship stuff. All I know was that she kept moving from guy to guy, and we kept moving for these men until we landed in Nana's house and Mom disappeared."

"How come she did the dumping, do you think?" Chance asked.

Sadie sensed the probing in that question. Just like Sadie had walked out on Noah…

"Mom was the kind of person who always thought things would be better somewhere else," Sadie said with a shrug. "I remember her telling me that she got itchy feet. She said I was better company than most boyfriends. Apparently not that good of company, though." A boyfriend had eventually won out over her.

She tried to sound like she was joking, but she wasn't sure she pulled it off. Chance didn't smile, and his gaze stayed locked on her face.

"Have you heard from your mom?" he asked.

"I found her," Sadie said. "In Denver."

"That's not far from here." He frowned, crossed his arms over his broad chest. "She was there the whole time?"

"Not far at all," she agreed. "That's the thing. I always hoped she'd come back. And that when she did, she'd have some excellent excuse for having been away for so long." She shook her head. "She didn't have much of an excuse."

"What's she doing now?"

"Working a part-time job at a Laundromat and telling anyone that will listen that she can stop the drug use anytime she wants—" She winced. This wasn't the kind of thing that people wanted to hear. It was ugly, painful. She'd told herself she'd keep her trap shut about this stuff. She was there to start her own business, and that wasn't achieved by airing personal laundry. She was trying to get some boundaries back again. But Chance wasn't a client, and he probably knew the most about her anyway, since any privacy she might have expected from Noah would have been expired once she walked out on him.

"I'm sorry," Chance said.

"Me, too." She shrugged. "But I can't fix her, and I can't make her into a decent mother. It is what it is."

That's what she'd told herself, at least. She'd had Nana, and that was a far sight better than being raised by a drug addict. Her mother had always been chasing a better guy, a better situation, another high. Maybe she'd been addicted to more than the drugs.

"Was she glad to see you?" Chance asked.

"She…" Sadie sifted through the jagged, painful memories of those awkward visits with her mother. "She asked me for money a lot. At first, I'd give it to her because I felt so sorry for her, but I knew what she was doing with it. And I couldn't keep it up. When I started saying no, she'd get angry. She'd do anything for her next fix."

Chance's expression had softened and he nodded slowly. "Are you still in contact?"

Tears misted her eyes. What was it about her mother that made her yearn for the woman even when she knew her mother was bad for her? She'd been raised by Nana, and she'd been loved and supported. She hadn't suffered, but no matter how good to her Nana had been, there was a space in her heart that only her mother could occupy.

"I'm actually scared to call," she admitted. "I know she'll ask for money, and I'll say that I can't, and she'll—" Sadie sucked in a breath and blinked back the tears. Her mother had a way of saying the most cutting things when Sadie turned her down.

"But Mom didn't used to be like this," Sadie went on. "She wasn't like this. She liked to party a lot, but she was fun, and I remember that she'd do my hair for me in front of the big mirror in her bedroom. She wasn't like *this*."

"So, that's where you went when you left town," Chance said. "To find her."

"I needed to get some answers." She wasn't sure that Chance could understand all of this— not deep down. He came from the picture-perfect Morgans here in Comfort Creek. They all attended church and were supportive and kind. Chance and Noah came from a different kind of family than she did.

"No, I get that," he said with a faint shrug. "I'd have done the same if it were my mom."

"Yeah, but your mom is great." She shot him a wry smile.

"And your mom is still your mother," he replied, and she felt her smile slip. Why did he have to be so insightful?

"Yes." She swallowed back the emotion that tightened her throat.

"There are addiction centers and rehab places that could help your mother," Chance said. "I could give you some contact information."

"I know." She wasn't telling Chance all of this so he could fix it for her. In fact, she wasn't sure why she was telling him this at all. "I said that when she was ready to get some help to give me a call and I'd help her to check in to a rehab center not too far from where she lives. I think it's all I can do."

Chance nodded. "It *is* all you can do, Sadie. Besides prayer."

Prayer had gotten Sadie through those emotional meetings with her mother over the last couple of years. God had been by her side, and she truly believed that He had guided her back to Comfort Creek. Home—at least the only home she'd ever been able to lay claim to. Except even in the midst of Nana's love and encouragement, there had been a part of Sadie that couldn't completely settle there. Maybe it was the part of her that would always long for the affection her mother couldn't provide.

Chance's gaze had softened, and the little room had warmed with the two of them inside it. She'd told herself that she'd come back with her head held high and she wouldn't let it drag her down. She had her answers, and she needed to move on with her life. She wouldn't talk about it—that had been her resolution: silence. It was easier when she didn't have Chance Morgan asking her questions in that quiet bass of his.

Sadie forced a smile. "Sorry. I didn't really mean to talk about that."

"It's okay. I'd rather hear the truth."

Would he really? Because Chance didn't seem too open to the truth about her feelings for his brother. He seemed to prefer his ideals, and really, who didn't? The sound of Nana's slippered footsteps came down the hallway, and both Sadie and Chance looked toward the door as Nana poked her head into the room.

"I have sugar cookies in the kitchen," Nana announced.

"I should get going," Chance said, straightening. "Thanks all the same, Abigail. I'll have to take a rain check."

"Up to you, but I can't promise when I'll make them again," Nana said, retreating once more, and Chance and Sadie exchanged a look.

"She makes it sound like she never bakes," Chance said with a wry smile.

Sadie chuckled. "I know. Her threats don't hold much water."

It felt good to laugh with someone who knew Nana...who knew this town. These were the moments she'd missed the most when she'd been in the city—the inside jokes and the shared laughter with Chance. She'd missed Noah's family more than she missed Noah, and when he died, she'd been guilty about that. She still was.

It was nice to be home, though.

"I'll walk you out," Sadie said.

Chance needed to cut this visit short. He hadn't meant to get into the personal stuff about Sadie's mom, but he could feel the sadness emanating from her and he'd wanted to comfort her somehow. He couldn't hold her, but he could listen. He could only imagine what a mother's betrayal must feel like, and looking at Sadie as she pretended that it didn't stab as deeply as it did had given him the same jolt he'd felt when he saw her fall on the street.

There was a part of him that would always be looking out for Sadie—and it wasn't just the cop in him, either.

Abigail was back in her chair in the living room when they came out, sitting with her Bible on her lap this time, and seemed to have been in prayer.

"Good night, Chance," Abigail said. "Drive safe, now."

"Will do," he said. What was it about Abigail Jenkins that just made the world seem safer? She was the kind of lady whose very presence reassured the younger generation that there was good in the world still.

"Sadie," he began, keeping his voice low. He glanced toward the old woman in her rocking chair. This might not be the best time to talk.

"Yes?"

He smiled ruefully and glanced toward her grandmother again. "It's okay."

"Hold on." Sadie grabbed a blanket from the sofa and wrapped it around her shoulders, then plunged her feet into her winter boots. When he opened the door, she followed him out onto the porch and shut the front door behind her. She was already limping less, so whatever she'd done to herself when she fell mustn't have been too permanent.

Chance glanced toward the living room window. He couldn't see the old woman from where they stood.

All was still outside on the porch, and big, soft snowflakes drifted down, making the night even closer to absolute silence. Every sound was muffled by the falling snow. The porch light shone golden around them, and Chance could see the white of Sadie's neck exposed to the winter cold, and he reached forward and rolled up a fold of blanket to cover her a little better.

"What were you going to say?" she asked softly.

For the life of him, he couldn't remember. He just hadn't wanted the evening to end quite yet, and he'd wanted to offer something… friendship, maybe? None of it had been formulated into words yet.

"You aren't alone here, you know," he said.

"I know."

"I mean—" Why did this have to be so hard? He didn't know how to scrape it all together. "You've got me, too."

Sadie frowned, her expression uncertain.

"I missed you." He plunged on. "Maybe more than I had a right to."

Her breath hung in the air and she looked

up at him with sadness in that dark gaze. "I missed you, too."

"You should have talked to me," he said. "Before you left, I mean. You should have said something—yelled at me. Something…"

"It wasn't *you*, Chance."

Did he believe that? He wasn't sure. He'd been the one to come within a hair of kissing her the night before she dashed out on her wedding. Coincidences weren't that big.

"Are you cold?" he asked instead.

"I'm okay." She tugged the blanket closer, then nodded toward the yard. "I like this time of day—especially when it's snowing."

Chance remembered that—the way Sadie used to look out at the snow as it came down. She was the only person in this town who got excited at an early snowfall. He'd never been a fan of snow—it complicated everything. His driveway needed shoveling. There were more accidents, the cruisers needed their winter maintenance, and all the drivers suddenly forgot how to drive when the first snowflakes spun through the air. But Sadie—she didn't care about the rest. Never had.

"I *really* missed you…" The words were out before he could think better of them, and when she looked up at him in surprise, he felt heat rise in his face. He hadn't meant to say that. "You should have called. Emailed. You just vanished, and we were left with a gaping hole in our lives." *We.* Yes, it had been all of them, but he was talking about himself. "*I* was left with a hole in my life…"

It was the truth, and he'd already admitted to it. He'd more than missed her and he'd felt guilty about that. He should have been able to sweep her out of his mind and move forward out of solidarity with his twin, but he'd been in love with her. And while he knew that feelings didn't excuse poor behavior, in his defense, he'd muscled those feelings back for five years. One slip on a warm summer night before she was to marry his brother…couldn't that be forgiven?

"Oh, Chance… You and I, we—" She shrugged helplessly. "You were my best friend. Did you know that?"

"Was I? What about Harper?"

"Her, too, but…" She swallowed. "You understood me better."

"Not well enough," he said gruffly. "I didn't see it coming."

The snowfall thickened and they both looked out into the veil of snowflakes that seemed to pull a curtain around them, absorbing the noise from the streets distant, and blanketing them in.

"I didn't mean to cause such a mess," she said softly. "I really didn't."

"And I didn't mean to spook you. We're even." He smiled wanly.

"And I'm glad you missed me." A smile came to her face. "There's no shame in missing a friend, is there?"

Did that mean that she'd missed him, too? He wasn't sure he even wanted to think about that. But she'd been a part of his life—a part of his extended family in a way—ever since her engagement to his brother. And she'd taken a piece of him with her when she vanished. Maybe he shouldn't feel angry about that, but he had. Anger was easier to deal with than the complicated emotional stew it covered. She'd done wrong by Noah, but she'd also done wrong by him.

"Sadie, I know I messed up," he said quietly. "But after knowing each other for so long, after a wedding I worked my tail off to help put together... I deserved better than that."

She turned back, and as she did, she was closer than he expected, her blanket covered arms brushing against the open front of his jacket. She looked up at him, equally startled, but neither of them moved.

"I wasn't punishing *you*," she whispered.

"Sure felt like it. If we were friends, then why did you freeze me out like that? Why the silence?"

Her cheeks grew pinker, and then she sighed. "You reminded me of Noah."

That stabbed. Of course, Noah was their common denominator, but he wished that for once her thoughts about him could have nothing to do with his brother. Sadie shivered and he put his hands on her arms to warm them.

"I'm not my brother," he said gruffly.

A swirl of snowflakes blew onto the porch and settled onto her chocolate-brown curls. She was beautiful—more than beautiful, she was *back*. A large, fluffy flake settled onto a curl by her cheekbone, and he reached up to brush it away, but as he did, his eyes met her deep hazel gaze. Those pink lips parted as if she were about to say something.

"I know—" she began, but then her gaze met his and the words evaporated.

He didn't want her to associate him with Noah—not for everything. He and Noah might have had a brotherly connection closer than most because they were twins, but Chance was very much his own man, and when he looked at Sadie, it was the man in him that responded. Not the brother. Not the friend. Definitely not the buddy.

He didn't know how to say that—not without sounding like an idiot. And so he did the next best thing, and he closed those last few inches between them and caught her lips with his.

She froze for a second, and he put his hands on her cheeks, tugging her closer as his lips moved over hers, and she settled against his chest. It was then that he noticed she was kissing him back and he smiled ever so slightly. He wrapped his arms around her, giving her all the warmth he had, and he felt a flood of such immense relief to finally have her in his arms.

He'd regret this—that was a guarantee—but he'd also never forget it.

He broke off the kiss and let out a jagged sigh. "Sorry," he whispered.

Sadie licked her lips and took an unsteady step back. He hated that chill of winter air that flooded between them. It was like they were cocooned away on this snow-cushioned porch. Just two people in a snow globe. He cleared his throat.

"Just—" He swallowed. "I'm not my brother."

She laughed softly. "Okay. Point made."

"I'd better get going," he said.

She raised her shoulders against another chilly blast of wind. She was definitely cold, and he'd just kissed her. The reality of that was sinking in now. He turned toward the stairs.

"Good night, Chance."

How he'd missed her. Five years apart, and he was right back where he used to be—longing for the wrong girl. There was something about this porch that melted away his inhibitions, he thought wryly, but he knew that was an excuse. It could have been anywhere—that kiss had been coming for a long time.

Chapter Eight

Work was a great way to escape emotional turbulence, and Chance took full advantage of his job as police chief over the next three days. There was always paperwork that needed his attention, and he pored over it, managing to get a little bit ahead, even. He didn't normally manage that, but he needed the personal space that paperwork provided.

That evening on the porch with Sadie had shaken him more than he liked to admit. Kissing her had never been his plan. He needed to work with her—and that was where it needed to stop. He'd *never* had a right to cross that line, and the last time he'd even considered it, his brother's world had crumbled. How many times had Chance wanted to tell his brother the whole story and ask for forgiveness? But he never had because he knew his feelings for

Sadie were the deepest betrayal, and it hadn't been intentional. Chance would never have stolen his brother's girl.

Sadie Jenkins had a way of twisting a man's heart around her little finger, and then shaking him free. She'd done it to both of them, even though Chance had tried to hide it. She'd become his personal cautionary tale about what to avoid. Falling snow and a blanket wrapped around those slender shoulders changed nothing.

Today as he sat at his desk, thumbing through a stack of forms, he was frustrated. While the paperwork had effectively kept him closeted away in his office, it hadn't given him anything substantial to keep his brain occupied. Paperwork was mind-numbingly boring, and it allowed him ample opportunity to remember.

Chance's parents had always encouraged Chance and Noah to be their own men. As fraternal twins, they looked different—Chance being fair and blue-eyed to Noah's dark hair and brown eyes. Everything about them was different, except their taste in women…and it had set them up for more fights and head butting than anything else.

Chance could appreciate that they simply had different personalities. Chance was more quiet and introverted. His emotional world stayed safely locked away on the inside, while his brother was a classic extrovert and charmed his way into hearts all around town. And not just with single women. Men enjoyed chatting with him about the game or their cars. Older women loved to try to set him up with their younger relatives. Noah was fun. He made everyone feel like the center of his world, if only for a few minutes.

Chance had thought that Sadie was too young for either of them when Noah had asked her out the first time. She'd been in her early twenties and looked younger still. For the first time in a long while, they disagreed about a woman. But Noah hadn't let age deter him. Noah was smitten from the start, and he brought her with him to pretty much every family event they had, giving Chance plenty of time to get to know his brother's girlfriend. And he discovered what Noah already knew— she might look young, but she had maturity beyond her years. She was smart and funny, and when she looked Chance in the eye, his breath caught.

She's amazing, Noah had said. *She's the whole package, Chance. I'm going to marry her.*

For the first time, his brother was in love. Noah was a changed man. His flirting with other women stopped dead. There were a fair number of women around town who were mildly offended to suddenly lose Noah's flattering attention. The single women who had hoped that his flirtation might mean more had to give up on him. He had eyes for only one woman, and that had changed everything for Chance. Sadie was officially out of bounds.

Except Noah had been right about Sadie. She *was* the whole package, and the more time Chance spent with her as his brother's girlfriend, the stronger his feelings for her grew. It wasn't supposed to be that way. He was supposed to be able to embrace her as a future sister-in-law. It wasn't as if he'd ever made a move—shown her that he felt anything more than friendship—but there was something about that sparkle in her eyes when she smiled up at him, trying to crack his proper reserve. She'd always seemed to assume that it was the uptight cop inside of him that wouldn't let loose and she wanted to help him enjoy life a little more. She was wrong, though. It wasn't only a more reserved personality that kept his defenses up; he was hiding his true feelings for her. She was better off not knowing what really lay beneath that professional shell.

Noah knew Chance better than anyone, and

he'd nailed Chance's true feelings when he announced that he was going to propose.

What is wrong with you? Noah demanded. *You don't like her? Or do you like her too much?*

Nothing. Propose. She'll be thrilled. Chance had shot back. *I'm not stopping you.*

You never once said you were interested in her, Noah had said, hitting it exactly. *You never told me. That's on you.*

Chance wouldn't admit to feeling anything but brotherly happiness about that upcoming wedding, but Noah had guessed the truth. In return for Chance's good wishes and support, Noah had thrown every available woman in Larimer County in his direction. Noah billed him as his bashful brother working in law enforcement who needed a woman to help crack that shell. There had been a surprising number of women willing to take on the challenge, especially with Noah off the market.

You need a date to my wedding, Noah had said seriously. *That plus one had better be filled.*

Chance didn't have the heart to put a woman through that, though. He could hide his feelings for Sadie, but he couldn't do that *and* pretend to have feelings for another woman. It wouldn't be right. He was a Christian, and he firmly believed that God gave him the strength to do the right thing. He also believed in honesty. Hiding his feelings for Sadie was enough of a lie to live. He wasn't adding more to that. His plus one had remained empty, and it had been for the best. Noah had needed his support that day, more than anyone had ever anticipated.

Chance finished inputting the last file, then closed the folder and pushed it across his desk. He was plagued by guilt. His brother was dead, but he still felt like he was betraying him all over again. He had no business caving in to old feelings for Sadie rooted in the time when she was Noah's. He'd prayed last night that God would just turn these feelings for Sadie off, but God hadn't said yes to that one. And why not? Was this a test? Because if so, last night he'd failed miserably.

His desk phone rang, and Chance picked it up.

"Sir, there is a call from Shelby West on line one."

Shelby West was Terrance West's mother. He'd been one of the young men who had died in the fighting overseas, and Toby Gillespie had contacted Shelby for information about her son. He closed his eyes and suppressed a grimace. Right now, complaints were the last thing he needed.

"Put her through," Chance said, and there was a soft click. "Mrs. West?"

"Hello, Chief. I'm glad I managed to catch you. I know you're busy."

"Not a problem," Chance said. "What can I do for you?"

"We had a visit from one of your officers yesterday," she said slowly. "An Officer Toby something. I think it started with a *G*. I wish I could remember, now..."

"Gillespie," Chance provided. "Yes, I know he went by. How did it go?"

"What a nice young guy!" There were tears in her voice, and Chance blinked. "I'm sorry." A sniffle. "He was just what my husband needed, Chief. That police officer was in the military, too, for a few years, and he could empathize with what Terrance would have gone through. He shared a few of his own stories about combat, and he...well, he just understood."

Relief flooded through Chance's shoulders and spine. This could have gone the other way. Was it possible that Toby's inner soldier had a place here in the force?

"I'm glad to hear that, Mrs. West," Chance said. "I'll be sure to let Officer Gillespie know that you appreciated the time he spent with you. We're going to try to do you proud in our ceremony coming up."

"I do appreciate that," Shelby replied. "Terrance deserves it. And tell that young man that if he ever wants a piece of pie and a coffee, he's to just come on by. He's always welcome."

"I'm sure he'll appreciate that, ma'am," Chance said. Probably more than she realized. "I'll pass along the message."

After they said their goodbyes, Chance hung up the phone and shook his head in silent amazement. He'd hoped that Toby would be able to soften his approach with these families, but he hadn't even dared to hope for a reaction this positive. God certainly worked in mysterious ways—that intimidating officer was exactly what a soft-spoken mother needed in her grief. And perhaps the Wests had been what Toby needed, too. Healing wasn't always a straight line, and everyone's path was a little different.

Including his own.

Sadie sat at the kitchen table, her swatches of American flag–inspired ribbon laying in front of her. It had been three days since she'd seen Chance, and she'd managed to nail down a printer for the booklets that would be handed out at the ceremony. She'd written up much of the content, but she still needed the personal information about the four soldiers. She'd been waiting for Chance to give her a call when he had the details, but so far he hadn't made contact.

She was feeling cautious, too, after that kiss on the porch. She'd gone over the details of the evening again and again, trying to pin down exactly what had happened, but she couldn't. All she knew was that in the close quiet of the falling snow, Chance had kissed her. It hadn't been a brotherly kiss, either. That was no chaste peck, and the memory of his lips moving over hers sped up her heart.

She'd never imagined that so much tenderness lay under that granite reserve. She'd seen a hint of it that night before her wedding when they'd come within a whisper of a kiss, but last night Chance had dropped that self-restraint, and she could still remember what it felt like to be held close in those strong arms, the scent of musky cologne tickling her nose. He'd said that he wasn't his brother, and that kiss had certainly proved it. She'd never been kissed quite like that. She exhaled a shaky breath.

But in some ways, Chance was no different from his brother. He was a good man with a lot to offer, and she was a woman with too many emotional issues at the moment. She'd always imagined herself different from her mother, but Lori had done the same thing— over and over again. She'd found a nice guy, settled down with him, convinced herself that he was worth it and then changed her mind. Sadie had never seen the fallout left behind by her mother's choices, and she'd been too young to really understand it all. But she'd never even suspected that she was like her mother when it came to romantic relationships, until she'd felt that rush of relief as she drove away from her wedding five years ago. And she couldn't do that to another good man—let him love her and then break his heart. A woman had a responsibility in these things, too. Sadie wasn't a houseplant or dish towel. She wasn't available to be swept off by whomever would claim her, and whether or not that kiss had left her breathless didn't matter. She'd almost married Chance's brother, and she wasn't taking any more risks with the Morgan family.

Sadie had a job to do here, and if three days

of going over that night on the porch hadn't resolved it in her mind, then another day wouldn't help. She needed to focus on what she could actually achieve. The mayor had a budget for supplies, and the wide ribbon that she preferred would bite into that budget more than she liked, but the others just weren't up to par. This was part of event planning—keeping the event affordable for her client—and Mayor Scott knew what he wanted. He might put up a casual, down-home kind of image, but underneath that public presentation was a detail-oriented perfectionist. Nothing shy of a bull's-eye for both image and budget would please him.

"I like that one," Nana said, pointing to a wide, crimson-and-white-striped ribbon, scattered with stars.

"Me, too," Sadie said with a wry smile. "It's the most expensive."

"So how is our mayor doing?" Nana asked, pulling out the chair next to Sadie and sitting down.

"He's made it very clear that if I don't do this his way, he won't be hiring me for his daughter's wedding," Sadie said. And she wanted that wedding—it would be a whole new level of accomplishment in her fledgling career path. Trina Scott's wedding would solidify her as a top choice for all of the who's who in Larimer County.

"His mother and I were good friends," Nana said. Sadie knew this. It was the personal connection that Sadie had with the mayor—the reason she'd been given a chance to begin with.

"I know, I know, and he used to give little speeches even as a child," Sadie said with a low laugh.

"He also used to steal cookies," Nana said, arching one eyebrow. "And he wet his pants in a silent revolt when he didn't get his way until he was six."

Sadie rolled her eyes. "We were all kids once, Nana."

While she hadn't been a pants-wetter, she had quite a list of naughty antics she'd gotten up to in her girlhood.

"I know, and we can forgive all those things because he was just a little guy, but he's now a grown man with the same tendency to have silent revolts." The older woman fingered the ribbon thoughtfully. "So keep that in mind, dear. He's a good friend to have because he can open doors for you all over the county, but Mayor Scott will be true to his word if you don't do things his way."

"I know." Sadie sighed. "But that's the business, isn't it? I'm here to bring people's wishes into reality. Everyone brings emotion to the table."

Including Chance. She pushed his face out of her mind. This wasn't supposed to be about Chance.

"And you're very good at this." Nana reached over and patted Sadie's hand. "I'm so proud of you. Let me fetch us some pie."

That was how most conversations with Nana ended, with a kind word and something to eat. Sadie watched her grandmother head over to the fridge, and then she put her attention back into the work in front of her. She didn't have a lot of time left. If she chose the more expensive ribbon, she might be able to cut costs elsewhere, but her order at the craft store needed to be submitted by morning to get it from the supplier in time and avoid extra costs.

But it wasn't the ribbon that worried her, it was the framework of the event. They mayor wanted an emotional, personal commemoration of the young men they'd lost. He wanted to show them as kids, as teenagers, as a part of the community and Sadie didn't have a right to do that with Noah's memory, especially not without Chance's blessing. She'd been a part of Noah's personal life, and when she'd walked away, she'd forfeited any right to use that personal connection to him. Except, the mayor was her boss in this, and she had to give him the ceremony he wanted. She was trapped.

Sadie pulled her laptop forward and opened the file for the booklet. She had to get this submitted to the printer, too, if they wanted a high-quality keepsake from the event. She glanced at her watch. It was half-past four, and he'd likely still be in the office.

"I'd better get that information from Chance," Sadie said. She couldn't wait for him to call her any longer.

"Should I give you some privacy?" Nana stood in front of the open fridge, a pie in her hands.

"We're professional contacts, Nana," Sadie said, standing up. That was as much as Nana needed to know, anyway. She pulled out her cell phone and Nana brought the pie to the counter. But as she dialed his number, she found herself wandering in the direction of the living room.

Nana looked out from the kitchen, a piece of pie on a plate, and she gave Sadie a small, secretive smile. Sadie rolled her eyes in return. If only Nana knew the half of it.

Sadie just needed to buck up already, act

like the competent woman that she was. Whatever happened on that porch had nothing to do with her job.

The phone rang and Chance picked up. "Chief Morgan."

"Hi, Chance, it's me… Sadie." She closed her eyes in frustration. She'd already called him by his first name, and this wasn't a personal call. "Chief, I mean."

"Sadie…" He paused. "Look, I'm sorry about the other night."

"Me, too."

"That one was on me," he replied quietly. "I've been thinking about it—"

"And avoiding me," she added.

He chuckled. "Maybe a little, but that was only because I needed to sort out why I did it."

"And why did you?" she asked.

"Poor judgment?" He sighed. "I was wrong. Let's just leave it at that."

Sadie swallowed. Poor judgment—the words every girl wanted to hear when she'd been kissed.

"I can do that," she assured him. "We'll just—not repeat it."

"Agreed." He sounded relieved. "I really am sorry, Sadie. This is all hard enough without any more complication."

"Chance, it's fine. I'm a grown woman. It isn't like I haven't been kissed before." Although, granted, she'd never felt quite so breathless afterward. She glanced toward the kitchen—had Nana heard that? Here was hoping she hadn't.

"So…anything I can do for you?" he asked.

"I'm just checking in with you about the personal details from the other men."

"Of course." His tone was turning professional again, and she wasn't sure if she was glad to hear the change, or not. They were better off on professional footing, but that kiss—while entirely inappropriate—had been personal. And she'd missed a personal connection to Chance.

"Have you managed to gather it all?" she asked.

"I have, actually." She could hear a rustle of papers. "I'm heading out in a few minutes. I promised I'd help my mom with the Wi-Fi. Why don't I drop it all by your place when I'm done there?"

"Is that a good idea?" she asked.

"I could have Cheryl scan it and email it over. She's working on a big project for a case, though, so it might take her a couple of hours to get to it." There was a pause. "Look, Sadie, we're going to have to work together, and I can promise you that I won't be crossing those lines again. If you'd prefer to work with someone else—the mayor maybe—"

"No, no," she interrupted. "We're both adults. I'm sure we can find a balance."

"Thanks." He sounded grateful. "That wouldn't look great on a report, I have to say."

Sadie smiled. True—he had a professional reputation to worry about, and kissing the event planner was frowned upon. "That would be nice if you could drop everything by. I'm on a tight deadline, so—"

"Point taken," he said, a smile in his voice. "I should be there about six. Will that cut into your dinner?"

"No, I'll have eaten by then. Nana's going out tonight, so it's an early supper."

"Okay. I'll see you then."

"See you." Sadie hung up her phone and looked down at it for a moment, wondering why she felt slightly ruffled after that conversation. The truth was, she was embarrassed by that kiss. She hadn't just been kissed—she'd kissed him back. Whatever feelings Chance inspired inside of her, she was responsible for her actions, and that embrace hadn't been right. She needed to keep her attention on her job and focus on the things she could control. Work made sense, and these jumbled feelings for Chance did not.

Chapter Nine

Chance's parents, Bonnie and Patrick Morgan, lived on the far south side of Comfort Creek in a little brown house at the end of a street. Their backyard opened onto an empty field that their dog ran through most of the day. Twenty-eight years ago, it was ten-year-old Chance and Noah wandering that field together, poking at stuff with sticks and talking about what they'd do when they were grown-up. They'd had a yellow Labrador retriever back then—Nancy. Chance had loved that dog...

Those walks had stopped when they got to be teenagers, when Nancy was an elderly dog and the boys had outgrown their romps. There was always a part of Chance's heart that saw the image of two young boys tramping across a snow-encrusted field when he looked out at it this time of year. Childhood was fleeting, but those boyhood memories had turned into a foundation for his and Noah's relationship. They were opposites in so many ways, but they'd always been brothers who could open their hearts and talk it out while they poked at things with a stick in the middle of a field.

Chance parked in the driveway of his childhood home and hopped out. The outside of the house hadn't changed too much over the years. There had been some fresh coats of brown paint—always brown—and a tree had been toppled by a storm in the front yard, but other than that, it was the same. The driveway was clear. His father had used the snowblower that morning, it seemed. Patrick Morgan was a handy kind of guy. If you gave him duct tape and a hammer, he was likely to fix whatever was broken, except the Wi-Fi—that still fell to Chance.

"Chance!" His mother opened the side screen door with a clatter. A black mutt dashed out behind her and met Chance with some chaotic licking and a wriggling rear end.

Bonnie Morgan was a petite, round woman with chin-length brown hair with only a hint of gray tucked behind her ears. She waited until Chance was finished with the dog before she added, "You're here."

"Miss me?" he asked with a smile.

"Always, sweetheart. Now please fix my internet." She wore a flower-print apron over her jeans and sweater, almost like an afterthought. She'd done that when he was growing up, too.

Chance followed her inside, the dog coming up behind. He kicked off his snowy boots and stepped into some slippers waiting for him. He gave the dog an extra pet while he was bent down there, anyway.

"You hungry?" his mother asked.

Chance headed into the den where the router was located. There was a faded couch in there, and a woodstove. It always smelled a little bit like fire, and he liked that. He bent down next to the familiar router and modem, and the dog flopped down on his bed next to the couch.

"I'll be okay," he said. "I'm dropping some papers by Sadie's place after this, so I don't want to take too long."

"Ah."

There was something in her voice, and he glanced over his shoulder. Her eyes had misted. That meant she was thinking about Noah, and that sparked more guilt. He'd wanted to bring those papers to Sadie himself because he wanted to prove that he could—that he'd had a weak moment, and that was it. He needed to prove it to himself, and to Sadie. If they were going to be coexisting in this town, then they needed to get that kiss behind them.

"Sadie and I have to work together on that remembrance ceremony, Mom," he said. "I don't have much choice."

Obviously, there was more to it, but not the kind of information a guy gave his mother.

"I know, I know…" She sucked in a breath and shrugged.

"Speaking of which—" he was reminded of the mayor's request "—they're wanting us to share some personal stuff about Noah. Childhood pictures, that kind of thing."

"Actually, that sounds really nice." His mother's expression grew sadder. "As long as you keep the spotlight off of your father and me. We don't want to do any speeches or anything like that. I don't think I could handle everyone staring at us—not at a time like that. So if you can do that much for me, I'll leave the rest up to you, son."

They shared that aversion to the spotlight during their grief. His parents had taken their son's death very hard. Susan Scott wasn't the only one who'd been crushed. They were both silent for a couple of beats.

"How is Sadie doing?" his mother asked.

An image rose in his mind of Sadie with that blanket wrapped around her shoulders, snowflakes caught in her chocolate-brown curls, and he quickly pushed it back.

"Fine," he said, more abruptly than he meant to. He unplugged the modem and the router, then sat back on his heels.

"Has she mentioned your brother at all?" she asked.

"She's talked about him a lot, actually."

"And?" Her expression was cautious, and he knew what she wanted to know. It was the same thing they'd been trying to figure out for the last five years: why had she left like that?

"She didn't love him enough," Chance replied.

"I guess we knew that much." Bonnie sank onto the side of the couch and watched Chance as he plugged the boxes back in. "Your brother was the only one who didn't."

"And me," Chance retorted. "Gotta say, I expected a bride that day."

Regardless of what happened the night before the wedding. She'd had five years of dating his brother, after all, and that should have counted for a whole lot more than his bumbling expression of his feelings.

"Well, hindsight is twenty-twenty, right?"

his mother said quietly. "You know, we should have let him cancel."

"What are you talking about?"

"That time Noah and Sadie had that big fight after the invitations went out. You talked him back into marrying her, remember?"

That wasn't fair, though. Couples had fights, and that didn't mean they stopped loving each other. Noah had been frustrated with all the wedding drama going on. There was something about Sadie wanting a smaller wedding, after all...

"You took him out for a coffee—"

"A steak, actually," Chance corrected her.

"—and you told him he'd be crazy to lose Sadie Jenkins."

That part was accurate. Noah had looked dismal sitting across that restaurant table. Everything about him had been deflated. Noah said that Sadie kept pulling back. She'd already suggested a couple of times that they just elope, but while she didn't have too much family in Comfort Creek, Noah did, and he couldn't just pare down the guest list without seriously offending a lot of people he cared about. Besides, Noah didn't want a wedding on a beach, he wanted a wedding in their local church, and contrary to popular opinion, a wedding wasn't only about the bride.

But Chance could also see that Sadie was the best thing that had ever happened to his brother. She brought energy and life into his brother's orderly existence. Noah's success in business could be attributed to his nitpicky attention to detail, but Sadie had shaken up Noah's world in a good way.

Chance had forgotten about that episode, though, and now that he was reminded of it, a surge of guilt rose up inside of him. He'd convinced Noah to go ahead with a doomed wedding, and he'd flustered Sadie the evening before the big event. If he'd just kept his distance, everything might have gone forward without a hitch. He was a worse brother than he'd thought.

"I think we put Sadie in a tough position," Bonnie said. "I don't think we gave her a way out. We were all so enthusiastic about that wedding. Maybe we were…too much."

The only thing that had been too much was *one* mistake on her porch. He wasn't going to take responsibility for the rest.

"Yeah, forgive us for being supportive." Chance nodded toward his mother's laptop. "Pass me your computer, Mom."

She handed it over, and Chance clicked through the start-up menu.

"We didn't give Noah much of a way out, either," Bonnie continued. "We all assumed that they wanted to get married, and we were excited about that. I mean, Sadie was delightful. We all loved her. Maybe a few more naysayers in our midst would have been good for those two. They could have had their convenient exit and then blamed us for the rest of their lives for having meddled."

And Noah might still be alive. He knew what his mother was thinking. She'd rather have him blame her for a failed wedding than have him dead.

Should Chance have seen this coming? Should he have read between the lines and helped his brother call the whole thing off? Chance wasn't going to encourage his brother to lose the best woman Larimer County had to offer because of his own jealousy. But looking back on it now, maybe if Noah had been able to end their relationship on his own terms, he wouldn't have felt chased out of town by the humiliation. And maybe if Chance hadn't been blinded by his own attraction to his brother's fiancée, he would have seen that.

"I honestly thought I was doing the right

thing by telling him to go through with it," Chance said.

"We all did." Bonnie shook her head. "Don't blame yourself, son. Most of the time families feel regret that they weren't more supportive. They see a couple who they think are doomed for marital failure and refuse to give their full support. And then the couple stays together and never forgets. You never think your mistake will be being *too* supportive, do you?"

But Chance had regrets of his own that his mother had no idea about. Like falling for his brother's fiancée. The Wi-Fi signal on his mother's computer popped up, showing that she was connected, and he passed the laptop back.

"Done," he said.

"Thank you, Chance." Bonnie put a hand over her heart. "You're a good son."

She'd always said that to her boys, and Chance still liked to hear it. He was a good son who took care of his mom's Wi-Fi. He'd just failed in being a brother. He glanced at his watch. He still had time.

"Maybe I'll grab a sandwich before I go," he said.

"Alright." His mother rose to her feet and the dog did, too, out of canine solidarity with his mistress. "I have some Crock-Pot mac and cheese, too, if you're interested…"

Being too nice wasn't what made Sadie walk away. That run from the altar was on Sadie… and possibly on him. But there was no way he could blame his mom.

Sadie heard the knock on the door from where she sat at her laptop in the kitchen. Her heart sped up a little, and she attempted to calm her nerves. They'd talked about that kiss, and they were moving forward professionally. Which was important, because she wasn't finished with Chance yet, either. She still needed to get his okay on the information she'd use for his brother. And, if she had to be brutally honest, she'd missed him.

As she pulled open the front door, Chance looked every bit the reserved cop. His shell was back in place, it seemed. A frigid wind whisked past him, curling around her legs, and Sadie shivered.

"Come in, quick!" she said, and when he did, she slammed the door shut behind him. She pulled her sweater a little closer.

"Hi." He had a manila envelope under his arm, and he handed it over. "As requested."

"Thanks." The envelope felt heavy. "I appreciate this. I need to get the write-ups done tomorrow so that I can get the booklets delivered to the printer."

Professional. She was rather proud of herself right now.

"Great. Glad to help." Maybe it was the uniform that did that—gave him some extra steel. "I should probably—"

"I needed to go over what you're okay with me sharing about Noah," she interrupted. "If that's okay."

"Right." He cleared his throat. "Sure. I could do that."

Sadie caught him looking at her, and when she met his gaze, his cheeks colored slightly and he looked down. This was hard for him, too, she realized. If they could just get past it... But first things first. She needed his approval for *something*—some small piece of information he could give his blessing for. As Chance had said, they still needed to be able to work together, and neither of them wanted to tell the mayor that they couldn't keep it professional.

Chance hung his coat on a peg and stepped out of his winter boots. He followed her through the living room, into the kitchen, and she could sense the bulky comfort of his presence behind her.

Sadie dropped the envelope on the table. "Are you hungry? There's some leftover blueberry pie."

"Your grandmother's pie is hard to turn down," he said with a grudging smile. "Sure."

Sadie dished him up a slice. When she turned around, she caught Chance's gaze on her again. His blue eyes met hers for a moment, and then he accepted the plate.

"Are we okay?" Sadie asked cautiously.

"As far as I'm concerned," he said with a nod, but there was a flicker of something softer in his eyes. Was that friendship? She felt a wave of relief so strong that she had to blink back a mist of tears.

"Because I don't want to change things between us," she added. "I miss us getting along. Buddies might be too much to hope for, but I liked where we were at before."

"Yeah, me, too," he agreed. "We're okay, Sadie. I promise."

She pulled open a drawer for a couple of forks.

"So I just came back from my parents' place," Chance added.

Sadie had really liked Bonnie Morgan. She'd have been the ideal mother-in-law. She loved her boys dearly, but she had a very balanced view of them, and she wasn't one to push into their relationships. She'd been funny, too, and chock-full of marriage advice gleaned from a very happy, forty-year marriage.

"So how do they feel about this ceremony?" she asked.

"My mom was the one I talked to, and she's okay with it." Chance took a bite of pie and swallowed before he spoke again. "She just doesn't want the spotlight on them. They don't want to do any speeches or anything like that."

Did that change things for Chance? she wondered. She watched him as he took another bite, his expression grim. Sadie put her plate down on the table and opened the envelope. She sorted through the contents—some pictures of each man, a write-up of their personal histories and their service in the military. There seemed to be some anecdotal stories included in different handwriting. When she got to Noah's information, it was sketchy—his military information and one picture of Noah in uniform that Chance must have provided.

Her heart stopped for a beat as she looked down at the familiar face. Noah had been a handsome man—and that photo brought back his memory in a rush so hard that it brought tears to her eyes. She might not have been the right woman to marry him, but she had loved him.

"When I left your brother, I honestly thought that I'd have to face his life without me," she admitted. "He'd meet someone new—or someone who'd been waiting in the wings. Then I'd come home to visit, and I'd see Noah with his wife and his kids. Maybe in the grocery store, or in a park. I'd drive past the house I was supposed to share with him, and I'd have to find a way to deal with everything I gave up."

"And you were okay with it?" Chance asked.

"I dreaded it." She smiled sadly. "But given the alternative, I wish I could be in that uncomfortable situation instead."

"You and me, both," Chance agreed.

They were silent for a couple of beats, and then Sadie pushed back her melancholy. They had work to do, and she had deadlines.

"Okay, well, we need a few memories of Noah that we can share during the ceremony. We're going to have some personal stories that show the kind of men they were. You said your mom wants to keep out of the spotlight, right?"

"Yeah."

"I'll make sure anything that's read from the front doesn't come from family. That will keep your parents out of the middle without being obvious."

"Thanks for that."

"But I'd need to have something I can share about Noah." She leaned forward. "Something you'd sign off on, so to speak."

"I understand why this is necessary, but I still don't want a lot sentimental outpouring about Noah." Those icy blue eyes met hers again. She sighed—he'd been abundantly clear.

"Which is why I'm coming to you. I'm trying to do this right, Chance."

Could he see that? She didn't want to disrespect him, but she had a job to do. Mayor Scott had made his wishes very clear.

"Okay…" He dropped his gaze and nodded. "I get it. The mayor has you in a tight place right now."

She felt a wave of relief. "He really does, Chance. Thanks for recognizing that. So, let's think of some memories of Noah that can show this town the kind of man he was while still respecting your privacy. It's a fine line, I know, but I think we can do it."

Chance took another bite of pie. "He was involved in Big Brothers. That's something he cared about."

"Yeah, I remember that." She clicked a pen

open and jotted it down. "Didn't he also help reroof a couple of barns that year with the terrible wind storm?"

"Yeah, for free, too." Chance nodded. "He was a good guy."

"That was the year you and Noah started work on that boat, remember?" she asked, a smile coming to her lips. "You were going to fish together all summer. He said I could fry up your catch, and I told him he could fry up his own catch. I don't scale fish."

Chance smiled sadly. "Yeah, we didn't get too far, though. Neither of us knew anything about refinishing old boats. I doubt it would have floated once we were done with it, anyway…" Chance paused. "We said we'd buy a decent boat new. We said we'd take Dad fishing."

They wouldn't have had the chance to do it, she realized. Noah left for the army shortly after the wedding fiasco.

"I'm sorry, Chance," she said softly. "It would have been fun."

Chance nodded and looked away. A tear sparkled in his eye and he blinked it back. This was fresh for him.

"I should have seen it coming," Chance said, his voice gruff. "He should have told me he was thinking about the army. But he wouldn't have—" He stopped.

"I don't get it," she said. "Why not? You two were so close. I don't understand why he wouldn't have brought it up, especially since he'd obviously gotten serious about it. You were his twin brother."

"Because he and I—" Chance stopped, cleared his throat. "He knew how I felt about you." Chance met her gaze with an anguished expression and he scrubbed a hand through his short hair.

"What?" His words sank into her mind. "Noah knew?"

She'd assumed that Chance had managed to keep that secret from Noah, as well. She certainly hadn't clued in until the night before the wedding when he'd finally said something, but even then...

"That's why he didn't tell me anything. I'd harbored some pretty intense feelings for you, and I don't blame him for not believing he could trust me. He wanted to start a life with you, and knowing how I felt, he needed to take a big step back from me."

Chance had been distant, so reserved. She'd spent more time than she should have chipping away at that professionalism of his, and all that time he'd been hiding deeper emotions than she'd ever imagined. In that light, her teasing and cajoling had been far from appropriate.

"You just said that you'd be interested if I changed my mind about Noah…" She searched through her memories. "It was a crush, I thought."

"Maybe a bit more than that." Chance shook his head. "You two fell in love, and I sorted out my feelings privately. That's how I do things, if you hadn't noticed."

And she'd spent years—literally years—cozying up to her future brother-in-law, never realizing how difficult she was probably making it for him.

He met her gaze once more, and she saw a flicker of a smile on his face. "I was the biggest champion of that wedding. Would have been nice if you'd actually gone through with it."

They were silent for a few seconds, and Sadie's heart welled with regret. She'd noticed some tension between the brothers, and she'd chalked it up to Noah getting married. Marriages changed dynamics, and she'd done her best to keep the brothers close. They needed each other—she wasn't one of those women who tried to take a sibling's place in her man's heart.

She'd been so naive back then…and because of Chance's feelings for her, he hadn't been close enough to his brother to be taken into confidence. While she hadn't intended that, or even suspected, she had spent several years trying to draw the man out of his shell, trying to bond with him despite his reluctance. And because of that, Noah wouldn't confide in the brother who might have made all the difference.

"And now?" she asked hesitantly.

"Sadie, that's all in the past," he said. "You have nothing to worry about."

"But the…um—" She swallowed. *The kiss.* That's what she was trying to say and kept getting stuck in her throat. Chance raised an eyebrow.

"You mean the other night. Just a little nostalgia. It's under control." Those blue eyes met hers once more, and then he heaved a long sigh. "Trust me on that."

"Okay." She nodded.

"So back to business."

She had questions, but she wasn't even sure what they were right now, or if she should even ask them. Whatever his feelings had been, if he said he'd dealt with them, then she had to believe him. And he was right—they needed to focus on the work at hand.

"Yes, back to business." She sucked in a wavering breath and looked at her notes. "So we can mention the Big Brothers program, the barn reroofing…and the boat?"

"No." Chance's tone hardened. "Don't mention the boat. That's private. Use the other stuff. And if you have a memory with Noah, use that."

"Should I ask one of your cousins, maybe? Would that make things easier?"

"No, just keep it simple."

He sounded tired, and she circled the options on her notepad, then looked up at Chance once more.

"I'm sorry, Chance," she said softly. "I wouldn't have come between brothers. You know that, right?"

"You didn't." He fixed her with a granite stare. "And I was fine. It was under control. There's right and there's wrong, Sadie. Feelings don't change that."

She didn't answer. Noah hadn't been the jealous type, but whatever it was that Chance had felt, it had been enough to drive a wedge between the brothers.

"I'm going to head home," Chance said. "You have what you need from me?"

"Maybe a few more photos of Noah," she said.

"I provided one."

"Right." That was as much as he was going to give on that front, and she wasn't about to push it further.

He paused with a hand on the back of the kitchen chair he'd just vacated. "I hope I haven't made you uncomfortable."

"No, of course not." That wasn't exactly true, but it was the polite response. "I appreciate you coming by."

"Good night." The wall was back up—that shell he always hid behind. And maybe there had been a better reason for that personal shield than she'd given him credit for. It was time to step back and leave Chance alone.

She'd inadvertently gotten between Chance and Noah in life, and she couldn't allow herself to do that now that Chance was grieving his brother's death.

Lord, she silently prayed. *What did I do?*

Chapter Ten

The next morning, Sadie sat with a cup of coffee in front of her, watching the snow fall outside the kitchen window. She could hear a neighbor shoveling a driveway, the metal scraping against asphalt and carrying in the midmorning air. She'd gotten up early and had already done a lot of the writing for the booklets to be printed. Her eyes ached from the long time in front of the computer screen.

Nana had gone out to buy some nutmeg. She had more baking plans, apparently, and Sadie heaved a sigh. Pumpkin pie, or whatever it was on the menu, wasn't going to ease her disquiet this morning. Her mind was still on Chance's revelation the night before: he'd had feelings for her. That night on the porch before the wedding had been more than an articulated crush—it had been much more...

Had she really been so stupid not to see it? She felt naive this morning. She hadn't been a slip of a girl, so she didn't feel like she had much of an excuse. She'd been twenty-two when she and Noah started dating, and twenty-seven by the time they were supposed to get married. How on earth had she missed something like that?

If it weren't for her good-natured pestering of her future brother-in-law, if she hadn't been blithely enjoying his company instead of focusing on the romantic relationship with Noah that she was supposed to be invested in... If she'd looked closer at what she had with Noah sooner instead of avoiding the hard topics by hanging out with his family, she might have broken it off before she'd done so much damage. At the very least, she might have been less of a wedge between Noah and Chance. In the end, Noah hadn't needed *her*, he'd needed his twin brother, and he hadn't had that fraternal relationship because she hadn't been taking anything seriously enough!

And now she was asking Chance to share precious memories of his late brother in order to please the mayor. Yet again, she felt like the wedge, this time between Chance and his brother's memory. She hated that—it had never been intentional. Just like her mother…blithely breaking hearts in her path as she swept off to whatever new horizon tugged at her. When a man like Noah could offer her everything and it still wasn't enough, then the problem wasn't the man—it was inside of her. Was she destined to live a life of constantly seeking, like her mother had, leaving heartbreak behind her?

But if Sadie didn't plan this ceremony to the mayor's specifications, she stood to lose a great deal. Still, was the mayor's good word worth putting Chance through all of this? She might have been terrible for both Noah and Chance, and maybe it was time for her to sacrifice something for them and make up for all the pain she'd caused.

She'd been praying about it all morning, and God didn't seem to be answering yet. God had been so clear about her move back to Comfort Creek. He'd come so close that there wasn't a doubt as to what she should do. She'd felt His nudge as clearly as if He'd taken her by the hand and led her back home. So why the silence now?

Sadie had only had one mug of coffee so far, and she needed a whole lot more caffeine to keep herself rolling today. She pushed to her feet and brought her empty mug to the counter. She wasn't quite ready to get back to work yet. She'd set herself a personal deadline of completing the write-ups today so she could get everything uploaded to the template tonight and get her order in line for printing. The clock was ticking on this one.

She reached for the coffeepot, and as she did, she saw a bundle of envelopes behind the coffeemaker. Normally, she wouldn't bother with her grandmother's stashes of old mail, but she noticed some red lettering on the front of one envelope, and she tugged it out. It was an electricity bill with the words "Final Notice" emblazoned across the front. She froze, then grabbed the rest of the mail in a single handful and pulled it out.

As she flicked through the envelopes, she saw more of the same—unopened bills. Sadie tore open the most recent phone bill and saw that her grandmother hadn't been making her payments lately and she owed a good amount of money. She didn't have her service cut off yet, but she was definitely in the hole. The same was true for her electricity bills and the natural gas. The only thing she seemed to be up to date on were her property taxes, which was a relief, considering.

How long had this been going on? Her heart thumped hollowly in her chest. Her grandmother had never hinted that she'd been having money problems, and Nana had been so happy that she'd been coming back, and showed her joy with treats and baking. If she'd ever even suspected that she'd be a burden—

Sadie heard the sound of footsteps on the side walkway, and she guiltily looked up as Nana turned the knob. She was tempted to push the envelopes aside, but she couldn't pretend she hadn't seen these.

"So I ran into Linda across the street—" Nana began, and then stopped short as her gaze fell onto the pile of envelopes. Her cheeks were already pink from the cold, but her gaze flickered away from Sadie and she shut the door solidly behind her.

"Nana—" Sadie began.

"Linda's grandson is joining the army," Nana went on, but her tone had changed. She was embarrassed, Sadie could tell.

"Nana," Sadie repeated. "We have to talk about this."

"No, we don't," her grandmother replied with a shake of her head. "Put those back where you found them and stop snooping, young lady."

If only it were so simple. She wished she could do that and let Nana off the hook. She hated embarrassing her, but this was a big problem, and ignoring it wouldn't fix anything.

"I didn't know you'd been falling behind," Sadie said. "You should have told me. I could have been helping you out."

Sadie had been picking up groceries, but her grandmother had refused to take a penny toward other expenses. Did Nana really not have enough money coming in to pay her basic bills?

"I don't need help," Nana said, shaking her head. "It's fine."

"It isn't," Sadie said. "Nana, I'm not a child anymore. I'm thirty-two! I can pitch in. We'll sort this out."

"You need to focus on starting up your business," Nana insisted, shooting her an arch look. "I'll catch up. I always do."

"So this has happened before?" Sadie asked quietly.

"Once or twice. God always provides, dear. Now, you have your business to worry about. That's important to both of us. I'll take care of the rest, Sadie. Put together that ceremony and impress the socks off of the mayor."

"Nana, you need some help *now*. I can pay some of these bills—"

"With what?" Nana made it sound ridiculous, and Sadie shook her head.

"With the nest egg I set aside for my business. I'm not going to sit on money while you're struggling, Nana! You raised me better than that."

Her grandmother pulled a bottle of nutmeg out of the grocery bag in her hand and put it on the counter with a thunk, then balled up the bag in her hand and shoved it into another grocery bag hanging from a cupboard door handle.

"No!" Nana's soft tone hardened. "You can chip in a little once you get paid for this job, and not a minute before. Do you understand me? That money is to give you a fair start at your own business, and I like that bigger picture. You've finally found your calling, and I'm not going to derail you. I've held out this long, and I can hold out a little longer still."

"They'll turn off our power," Sadie warned.

"I pay a little each month. They won't cut my power yet," Nana said with a shake of her head. "Now you stop worrying about my finances and get to work on that ceremony. I think we both know that our mayor won't accept anything but the best." Nana turned toward the living room. "Now, I'm going to go warm up my feet, if you don't mind, dear. I'll let you get back to work."

Was that it? That was all the discussion Nana would give to her situation? Sadie didn't know what she'd expected, but it was more than that.

"Nana—" she called.

Nana disappeared around the corner, but her voice filtered back. "And put those envelopes back where you found them."

Sadie sighed. Nana had always been a proud woman, but she'd never suspected that her grandmother was struggling to pay bills. She wished she'd known that sooner. To think she'd been stashing away her own little nest egg of cash to fund her small business while her grandmother had been falling behind. Sadie had money in the bank right now, while her grandmother was pinching pennies. That stung. Sadie had wanted to rent an office space here in Comfort Creek, but that would all have to wait. Her priorities had just reshuffled.

Nana was going to need more than an injection of cash to pay off her debt; she was going to need some ongoing help to stay afloat. Sadie had come home to start a business, but it looked like she'd be providing for more than just herself, and she needed to start getting a regular income right away. This project for the mayor just became a whole lot more important.

She might be willing to sacrifice her own plans to make up for the pain she'd caused Chance and his family, but Nana needed her now. This job might be painful for Chance, but it was the start she needed to begin supporting Nana. Sadie couldn't afford to lose it.

Chance slowed his pace on the snowy sidewalk as he came upon the owner of the stationery store, Vern, shoveling his section of sidewalk. The snow was still coming down in slow, lazy flakes, and the sidewalk had a white velvet covering up until the stationery store where Vern was keeping it completely clear. A short, black man with a balding head and a friendly smile, Vern was a fixture around there.

"Morning, Chief," Vern said, giving his shovel a knock against the cement.

"Good morning."

Vern let him pass, then continued shoveling with the scrape of metal against sidewalk. Chance's mind had been preoccupied ever since last night. He hadn't meant to say so much—what was with him lately? He'd spent five years bottling up his feelings around Sadie and never letting on that he felt anything besides casual friendship, or perhaps a bit of a crush, and now that the pressure was off, he'd suddenly announced it, and all its messy glory.

And she'd looked stunned.

Lord, what is with me? I keep praying for guidance and discretion, and I keep blowing it.

God normally answered those prayers for him and he was able to keep a lid on his feelings, so why was God suddenly leaving him alone in this?

Chance was frustrated with himself. It didn't matter what he'd felt all those years ago. This was now, and she still wasn't the right woman for him. He was clear on that, but he couldn't help the way he felt when he saw her in her kitchen last night. It was the same way he'd felt since the beginning. But those feelings for Sadie had been the cause of everything that led to his brother's death—so why couldn't he stamp them out?

The door to the drugstore opened, and Randy Ellison came out onto the sidewalk. He wore a winter jacket open in the front, and his hands were plunged into the pockets. He nodded at Chance, his breath coming out in a cloud in the cold air, and then the door burst open again and Bob Litton hollered, "Stop him! Thief!"

Chance didn't have to do any stopping, because Randy turned back, rage written all over his face.

"What are you talking about?" Randy demanded. "I didn't take anything."

"Two chocolate bars," Bob snapped. "Check his pockets."

"I put them back!" Randy took a step back. "I didn't take anything."

"Two chocolate bars," Bob repeated, crossing his arms over his chest, glaring at the teenager. Vern stopped his shoveling and stood watching the scene with a conflicted expression. Chance sighed. Randy and his brother Burke had been caught shoplifting in the past, so it wasn't unheard of. And Bob didn't accuse lightly.

"You sure, Bob?" Chance asked.

"I saw him with them, myself," Bob retorted.

"Randy, I'm going to pat you down, okay?" Chance said. Randy's answer was a baleful glare, and Chance gestured for him to put out his arms.

"Seriously?" Randy rolled his eyes, but did as he was told. Chance patted his pockets, his sides, the front and back of his coat.

"Nothing, Bob," Chance said with a shake of his head.

"What did I say? I put them back." Randy's mouth twisted with distaste, but Chance caught a mist of tears. The boy was embarrassed, and rightfully so.

"Fine." Bob looked a little embarrassed, too, but he'd been robbed by schoolkids for years, and Randy had been one of the most successful shoplifters. So Chance didn't exactly blame him this time around.

"Sorry about that, Randy," Bob said. "But you've done it before—"

"I put them back!" Randy's voice went up, and Bob shook his head and turned back inside. Randy spun around to leave, too.

"Randy, wait," Chance said.

The teenager turned back, his expression bitter. "What?"

"I'm sorry about that, too," Chance said. "I had to check."

"Yeah. I got it." He took a couple of steps backward. "Just keeping law and order. So I can go now?"

Chance glanced in Vern's direction and the man quickly turned his attention to shoveling the last of the snow off his stretch of sidewalk.

The kid was embarrassed, and Chance felt

a wave of regret. He was pigeonholed already, and that kind of stigma had a way of being a self-fulfilling prophecy.

"Let me buy you a hot chocolate," Chance said.

"I'm not a ten-year-old," Randy snapped.

Chance smiled wryly. "Fine. A coffee, then."

Randy thought for a moment, then shrugged. "Sure. Whatever."

It was the middle of a Friday morning, and rightfully the kid should be in school, but Randy had bigger problems than truancy right now. They walked together to the next shop over, The Daily Grind. It had some of the best hot chocolate Chance had ever tasted, made from whole milk, melted dark chocolate and topped with a dollop of whipped cream. But hey, if the kid wanted a black coffee in order to act older, Chance would let him choke it down.

They went inside and Chance bought them each a coffee and then led the way to a table in the far corner. Randy sat down and stared into his cup morosely.

"So how was the AA meeting?" Chance asked, keeping his voice low.

"I went."

"I know," Chance replied. "I checked. How was it? What did you think?"

"I don't know." Randy looked up. "Those people seem like they have problems."

"And you don't?" Chance asked.

"Not that I have to talk about," Randy said.

Yeah, that's what Chance thought, too, last night, and then he'd started talking. It could be both healing and humiliating at once. He knew that feeling.

"But you went, that's our deal," Chance said. "Keep going. Every week."

"I'm not a loser," Randy said, taking a sip of his coffee. "Contrary to popular opinion around here."

"Do you think I see you as a loser?" Chance asked.

"You patted me down, didn't you?"

That was because he'd suspected that he was a thief—maybe not too far off.

"Thing is, Randy, everyone in this town knows you," Chance said slowly. "They know your mom and your sister. They know the stuff you did as a kid to get into trouble, and they know your recent stuff, too. You've got a reputation around here, and you know it."

Randy was silent.

"I don't think you're a loser," Chance said. "But it's going to take some convincing for the people in Comfort Creek to see you as something other than a troublemaker."

"When all I have to do is walk into a store and Bob Litton assumes I'm stealing something—"

"You *have* stolen from him in the past," Chance reminded him.

"That was because I needed some cold medicine for my mom," Randy snapped.

Chance nodded. "I know." He paused, unsure of how much he wanted to share, but his brother had been filling his memories lately, and maybe some of Chance's mistakes could help Randy. "When I was your age, my brother and I went to a big party. It was at this girl's house, and her parents were out of town."

"You rebel," Randy muttered.

"Shut up and listen," Chance retorted. "I was only there to look out for my brother. I had the best of intentions. This girl's parents were incredibly strict, and the minute she got any freedom, she was acting up. Anyway, the girl's parents called in the middle of the party, and she said that she only had a couple of friends over. She named me, because her parents thought I was a nice guy, and she passed the phone over. She was silently pleading with me to back up her story, and I didn't want to get her into trouble. Her parents tended to punish pretty harshly. I thought I was protecting her."

"So you lied to them," Randy guessed.

"I did. I said it was just me and my brother and a couple of others and we were watching a movie. They believed me and hung up."

"And you couldn't live with the guilt?" Randy asked wryly.

"That girl ended up having a pill slipped into her drink, and she almost died that night. She was in a coma for several days, and there was some brain damage as a result. The point of my story is that we can have the best of intentions, but wrong is still wrong. My brother and I never should have been at that party, and I never should have lied to her parents. There are consequences for stupid choices, regardless of our intentions. And I know that firsthand."

Randy nodded slowly. "Got it."

Did he? Because life lessons were best learned by taking advice, not by going through it all the hard way.

"Now, I was sixteen and had a pretty good reputation, but I lost a lot of people's trust that night at the party. And I had to earn it back. That's not easy, but it's possible."

"So how exactly am I supposed to convince anyone I'm not some little thug?" Randy asked, and while his tone was harsh, Chance could see the pleading in those eyes. Randy actually wanted to know.

"You'll have to see yourself differently first," Chance replied. "And that will start with a real honest look inward."

"My name is Randy, and I'm an alcoholic?" he asked bitterly.

"How long since you last drank?" Chance asked.

Randy didn't answer, and Chance had an idea what that meant.

"Give those AA meetings a chance, Randy," he said quietly. "You can turn things around. It'll take some time, but people will start seeing you differently. I can promise you that."

Randy took another sip of coffee.

"And you're going to need your high school diploma," Chance added.

The teenager raised one eyebrow. "So I can be anything I want when I grow up?" His tone was sardonic.

"No." Chance leveled him with a no-nonsense stare. "That's just for a basic job. If you want more than a basic job, you're going to need some training. And no one in this town can chase you down and make that happen. You'll have to choose it."

"Yeah, yeah…" Randy muttered.

Chance sighed and stood up. "Thanks for the chat. Let's do it again."

"Do we have to?" Randy smiled wryly. The kid wasn't done with the attitude, apparently, but Sadie had taught this boy in Sunday School, and she saw more in him than anyone else in Comfort Creek did. Randy had one champion who still saw the potential in him.

"You could have taken the hot chocolate, you know," Chance said with a chuckle. "Unless you really do like that black coffee."

Color rose in Randy's cheeks.

"You aren't starting from scratch here, Randy. I wouldn't bother taking this time with you if I didn't think you had potential. And I'm not the only one. Sadie Jenkins thinks you're a bright kid with a good heart. Maybe start with her—make her proud."

"Miss Jenkins…" Randy's insolence melted away. "Yeah, I always liked her."

Was the key to Randy's cooperation as simple as the defiant Sadie Jenkins who demanded that he be treated with respect?

"School." Chance tapped his watch. "Now."

"I'm going." Randy smiled, ever so slightly. "See you around, Chief."

As Chance headed back out of the coffee

shop, he glanced at his watch. He had meetings today, and paperwork to get through. He had some sensitivity training to plan for other trainees. But still, Chance's heart was stuck on the woman he wasn't supposed to have loved. Looked like Randy might have been stuck on her a little bit, too.

Chapter Eleven

Sunday morning, Sadie sat next to her grand-mother in a wooden pew in the Hand of Comfort Christian Church. The late morning sunlight filtered through stained glass windows, dappling the carpet. Sadie dressed warmly this morning in a pair of gray woolen slacks and her cream cashmere sweater, but Nana was from another generation, and she wore a dress to church, no matter the weather. Sadie had offered to drive them, but Nana had refused.

"I like the walk to church," Nana said. "It reminds me of when you were little."

Sadie looked over the familiar people in front of her. Truthfully, she'd been scanning for Chance, but she didn't see him this morning. She did see other people she knew, though.

Lily Ellison—well, Lily Camden now that

she was married—sat a couple of rows up. She hadn't been in church last week, and Sadie hadn't seen her yet since she'd gotten back. Lily's husband, Bryce, was next to her, their dark-haired baby asleep on his shoulder. From what Nana had told Sadie, that baby girl had been left on the doorstep of the Comfort Creek police station that summer, and Lily and Bryce had ended up adopting her. Sadie couldn't help but smile as she looked at that peaceful little face. The baby sighed in her sleep, and Lily looked over at the infant as if by instinct. A lot had changed in the five years Sadie had been away—Lily was a mom, and married to a cop, while her brother, Randy, was out of control…

In the pew ahead of Lily and Bryce, was Lily's mother, Iris, and the twins, Carson and Chris. It looked like the oldest two boys weren't there…or at least not sitting with the family. She'd hoped that Randy would at least be at church, but maybe it was a bit much to expect from that age. She wasn't sure. Across the church, Chance's parents, Bonnie and Patrick, were seated close to the front, and next to them was her old Sunday school teacher who had long since retired from teaching the kids downstairs.

Before Sadie left town, she had been one of

three different youth leaders who pitched in at the church, and she wondered if she would want to volunteer in that capacity again. She'd have to wait until she had settled into her career a little more, but eventually she'd be contributing to her church. She always had. Churches ran best when everyone pitched in.

The service ended and there was the sanctuary-wide rustle as everyone stood to sing the doxology.

"Praise God from whom all blessings flow. Praise Him all creatures here below. Praise above ye heavenly hosts. Praise Father, Son and Holy Ghost."

Voices mingled into one choir as they sang the familiar, old hymn. Sadie loved the way her own unskilled voice could blend into something so much bigger and more beautiful. As the congregation split off into harmony for the final Amen, the pastor stepped back to the microphone.

"Don't forget that we're collecting for the Victims Fund for our local police station this Sunday. The collection box is in the foyer." The pastor smiled. "May God bless you all. Go in peace."

Sadie sat down to collect her purse and shot

her grandmother a smile. "It's nice to be back," she whispered.

Nana reached over and squeezed her hand. "I couldn't agree more."

From her seat two rows up, Lily turned around and shot Sadie a grin. "Hi!"

The people who had been sitting in the row between them moved toward the aisle, clearing a space for the women to talk.

Sadie leaned forward and squeezed her friend's hand. "Congratulations on everything—the wedding, your baby..."

"Thanks." Lily blushed, and her husband turned and smiled. Bryce had black hair and blue eyes—a striking combination that only served to make Lily look all the fairer next to him.

"I'd shake hands, but—" Bryce angled his cheek toward the baby. She moved in her sleep and Bryce patted her back. He looked like a devoted dad.

"No, no, it's fine." Sadie chuckled. "What's her name?"

"Emily," Lily said. "She's eight months, now. And she's back to waking up four times a night."

Lily and Bryce exchanged a wince, and Sadie smiled, but she sensed it was more of an inside joke between the couple. She felt a wave of longing. Lily had it all—the handsome husband, the new baby. She was definitely blessed. But Sadie had given that up, so it wasn't as if she hadn't had a chance at a life like Lily's. She could have stayed and sat in this very pew with her own handsome husband. Who knew—they might have had a baby by now, too. So feeling wistful about Lily's happiness wasn't fair on any level. Sadie had had her chance, and while it looked like a beautiful life from the outside, she knew her own wandering tendencies.

"Well, it's great to see you," Sadie said, rising to her feet. Nana had already left the pew and Sadie saw the back of her sweater disappear out the doors into the foyer. "I'd better get going."

Lily seemed occupied with the baby, so Sadie headed down the aisle in the direction Nana had disappeared. She paused at the door to shake the minister's hand and they exchanged a few pleasantries, so that by the time she got out in the foyer, she was just in time to see her grandmother tear a check out of her checkbook and slip it into the locked box marked Victims Fund. Sadie's heart sank.

"Nana," she whispered as she came to her grandmother's side. "What are you doing?"

"Oh, never mind," Nana said. "Let's go find our boots."

Nana didn't seem fazed at all by the fact that she didn't have enough money for her own bills, let alone charitable donations. She led the way to the coatroom, and Sadie bit her tongue while they got their jackets and changed into their boots once more.

When they finally got outside into the brisk air, Sadie said, "Nana, how much did you give?"

"The amount that I'd already decided upon weeks ago," Nana said, shooting Sadie a pointed look.

"How much?" Sadie repeated.

"Three hundred dollars."

Her stomach curdled. What was Nana thinking?

"But the bills—" Sadie protested. "There are enough people to contribute to the Victims Fund without you, Nana. You need to think about yourself a little bit!"

"It's going to be fine," Nana said with a shake of her head. "I have some money coming in, and it will cover the bills and this donation, too. I'm not senile, dear. It's a postdated check."

They headed back down the sidewalk, plastic grocery bags with their church shoes inside swinging at their sides. It was the kind of Sunday morning that would normally fill Sadie with peace and hope—their breath freezing in the air in front of them and sunlight sparkling on snow—if it weren't for her worries about her grandmother. She wasn't senile, she said, but she wasn't making some very stable choices at the moment. Was this a sign of how things would be from now on? Exactly how closely would Sadie need to be watching Nana's finances?

"What do you mean, there is some money coming in?" Sadie asked.

"I'm selling the dollhouse." Nana said it casually enough, and Sadie's heart clenched.

"You can't!" she gasped. "Nana, that dollhouse means the world to me."

"Dear, we can build another one," her grandmother replied gently. "We've been just tweaking that one for years now. It'll be fun to start fresh. Besides, a fully furnished dollhouse like mine is worth a great deal of money to the right person."

Yes, so Sadie had heard, but that dollhouse

had been an integral part of her own girlhood. She'd helped to decorate those rooms, to find the perfect accents and tiny details… She felt her eyes mist.

"Nana, I'll pay the bills," Sadie said. "I'd already decided to do it, but I wasn't going to say anything because I didn't want you to argue it."

"I don't need you to," Nana said firmly. "Are you going to start supporting my charities, too? No, dear, that's silly. I'm supporting that Victims Fund because I believe in it. And selling the dollhouse will take care of my bills. So you see, God always provides."

Except this provision was taking away a staple from Sadie's youth, and this hurt on a deeper level than she imagined possible.

"Nana, that dollhouse is a part of my childhood," she pressed.

"Aren't you going to ask me why the Victims Fund matters to me so much?" Nana asked, slowing her steps.

"I'd assumed it was because they did some presentation in church," Sadie said feebly. Wasn't that what usually happened? Someone put together an appeal that tugged at the heartstrings of the church members, and everyone opened their wallets. That was all fine and good for people who could afford to give, but it was an unneeded guilt trip for old women on fixed incomes.

"You should have seen the video they showed about the victims of crime," Nana agreed. "It's heartbreaking. We aren't the only ones who suffer in this world, and we've got to do what we can. But it's not just that, dear." Nana sighed and was silent a few beats, and then she went on, "I felt helpless."

"Helpless?" Sadie looked over at her grandmother, but Nana's gaze was focused on the sidewalk ahead of her. Sadie felt rather helpless at the moment, too. "Did someone pressure you?"

"No, nothing like that," her grandmother replied. "I've felt helpless for years. My little girl is addicted to drugs and there is nothing I can do about it." Nana's chin trembled. "That is the most powerless feeling there is."

"It isn't your fault," Sadie said.

"Perhaps not. As a mother, I've questioned that over the years—if I went wrong, pushed her too hard, didn't push hard enough. I did everything I knew how in raising Lori, but I went wrong, I suppose. And now that we know where she is, I still feel helpless."

"I know, Nana," Sadie said quietly. "I

couldn't help Mom, either. It isn't for lack of trying."

"But the thing is," Nana said, "I worship the Good Shepherd, and dear, He is a very, *very* good shepherd. He knows what he's doing, and He doesn't lose His lambs. Once upon a time, your mother was a little girl with a bright smile and she gave her heart to Jesus. And I believe that counts for an awful lot, Sadie."

A lot of good that did, Sadie thought bitterly. Her mother's life hadn't been an example of one well lived, as far as Sadie could see. She was an addict, she'd abandoned her only child and she now lived in squalor, waiting on her next fix.

"So I told the Lord that I'd leave my little girl in His capable hands," Nana continued, and her voice caught. "I'll trust the Shepherd to do what He does best, and go after her. While I wait on Him, I'll help the people that I *can* help. Like the Victims Fund."

"But the dollhouse," Sadie sighed.

Nana reached over and took Sadie's gloved hand in hers. "I know you love that dollhouse, but it's all I have that's worth anything right now, and it might be hard for you to understand, but I need to take care of my own debts, dear. I'm not your problem."

"You aren't a problem, Nana, but you aren't on your own anymore, either," Sadie said quietly. "But maybe you could give more of your time and less of your finances for a little while."

"The check is written, dear," her grandmother said firmly. "It's already done."

Nana's check had been slipped through the opening of a locked box, which meant it was safe for the time being. But first thing in the morning, Sadie was going down to the police station and asking for that check to be returned, and she wouldn't back down until Chance handed it over. Her grandmother didn't need to part with everything she held dear to appease her own guilt.

Chance rubbed his hands over his face. He'd come into the office early Monday morning to get some work done, but his mind wasn't on the piles of paperwork. He had been praying about Randy Ellison all weekend, but entangled with the present issue was the memory of Sadie's adamant defense of a boy she used to know. Her opinion mattered more than she thought. But Sadie's opinion wasn't the only formative one in this town, and he couldn't put the burden of a troubled teen onto Sadie's shoulders, either. No matter what he seemed to put his mind to this morning, he kept coming full circle again to Sadie.

Chance's office door stood ajar, and he heard the now familiar voice of his trainee saying hello to some officers as he ambled past. Good—he'd arrived. Chance had been waiting for him.

"Officer Gillespie!" he called.

The young officer returned and stood at attention in the doorway. His broad shoulders filled the space, and his expression looked like granite.

"Good morning, sir," Toby said.

"Come on in," Chance said, beckoning to the visitor's chair. "At ease. Have a seat."

Toby nodded and relaxed his stance, then slid into the chair Chance had indicated. "What can I do for you, sir?"

He still looked as impersonal as a tank, and Chance regarded the young officer for a moment while he considered.

"I have an idea," Chance said at last. "And I think you're the man for the job."

"Alright, sir."

"I want you to do a ride-along with Randy Ellison."

Toby squinted slightly. "The kid I arrested?"

"That's the one. He needs a goal, and I want to broaden his view a little bit." Chance paused. "Besides, he seems to like to skip school. We might as well make that time productive, don't you think?"

"I shouldn't bring him back to school?" he clarified. "Truancy is against the law—"

"I'm well aware," Chance said wryly. "But I want you to do this my way."

"With all due respect, sir, I don't think he likes me at this point."

Chance shrugged. "Most people don't like *him* at this point, either. I think we can work with that. Besides, I don't think he needs a gentle touch, this kid. He doesn't need long talks and sympathy, he needs a clear goal. I think this will work out well."

"And you want me to…" Toby looked questioningly at Chance.

"Show him what being a cop would mean," Chance said. "Show him what life would be like if he wore a uniform that demanded respect, and if he had a chance to make a real difference in people's lives."

"Doesn't he have a brother-in-law on the force?" Toby asked.

"Officer Camden. Yes. But that's family, and I'm not interested in fostering stronger family relationships—as positive as that may be. I want him to have an unbiased view that he can trust."

"And you want me to do this…now?" Toby asked.

"Well, first of all, I need you to swing by his house and get his mother to sign the permission papers, and then…yes. You'll see him around, I'm sure. Give him the option of a ride-along with you—in the front seat, of course—or being dropped off at the station to deal with me. I'm pretty sure he'll choose you."

Toby shrugged. "Yes, sir."

Chance slid the permission form across his desk, and the young officer picked it up.

"And for the record," Toby said, folding the page and tucking it in his front pocket, "you aren't looking for sensitivity and all that?"

"I'm looking for honesty and respect," Chance said. "We'll give sensitivity a break. Besides, I heard from Shelby West, and she was impressed with your demeanor when you visited them. She says if you ever want a piece of pie and a coffee, just drop by."

"Really?" Toby froze. "That's a high honor."

"It is." A smile toyed at Chance's lips. "So you have your orders for the day. I expect a full report."

"Will do, sir." Toby left the office, and Chance nodded to himself in satisfaction.

As long as Officer Gillespie wasn't arresting Randy, Chance had a feeling the two of them would actually get along. Toby wasn't the kind of man who could be manipulated by the kid, and Randy might actually respect a human tank, given the right circumstances. Randy and Toby could both get a win here.

His phone rang. It was Cheryl at the reception desk.

"Hi, Cheryl," Chance said, picking up the receiver.

"Sadie Jenkins is here to see you, sir," Cheryl said.

Sadie… He hadn't been expecting her, but his heart did speed up a little at the mention of her name.

"Send her in," he said.

Half a minute later, Sadie tapped at his door.

"Come on in," Chance said, rising from his chair. She came inside, undoing the front buttons of her woolen coat, and he noted the red spots on her cheeks from the wind outside. Her fingers looked red from the cold, too, and he had to hold himself back from reaching out to warm them in his palm. His instincts were all wrong here. Instead he leaned back against his desk and gestured for her to have a seat.

"You look cold," Chance said.

"I am." She rubbed her hands together. "But, no offense, the coffee out there looks like sludge."

Chance chuckled. "I have the good stuff here." He tapped his thermos. "Care for a cup?"

"You'd share?" She raised an eyebrow.

"Grudgingly." He grinned, then reached for a clean mug on top of his filing cabinet. He always kept two or three mugs there so that he wouldn't run out. He poured them each a cup of coffee and watched as she took her first sip.

"Chance, this is amazing," she said. "Thank you."

He sipped his coffee as well, and they were silent for a couple of beats before she added, "You weren't at church."

"Yesterday, I had to come in to the office. There was a domestic abuse situation outside of town, and lawyers were called in, so I was here all morning sorting that out."

"Oh." She nodded. "That sounds important."

"I take it you went," he said. He'd been thinking about her all morning, wondering if she'd been in church. He'd wanted to sit next to her...even though that was probably a bad idea. He was supposed to be keeping his emotional distance, wasn't he?

"I was there," she replied. "They had a collection for the Crime Victims Fund."

"It was successful this year," Chance said with a nod. "That money will help a lot of people."

"Yeah, well, my grandmother put in a check," Sadie said, lifting her eyes to meet his. "And I need that check back."

Chance frowned. He had a feeling Abigail wasn't going to like that. "What's going on?"

"She's giving money she doesn't have," Sadie said, and he caught a tremor in her voice. She was upset.

"She's never been the type to be forgetful," Chance said. "How old is she now?"

"She's seventy-nine," Sadie said, "But it's not about senility. I discovered a whole pile of unpaid bills. She's been falling behind. I guess her pension isn't cutting it. So she decided to sell the dollhouse, and she was going to use the money to pay off her debt and cover that check."

"She can't afford that, then," Chance concluded.

"No." Sadie dropped her gaze. "She can't."

"Look, don't worry about it," Chance said.

"I'll go find her check myself and remove it from the batch."

"Thank you." Sadie took another sip, and she looked like she was trying to pull her emotions back under control.

"Is Abigail going to be okay from now on?" Chance asked. "I mean, if her pension isn't enough to pay her bills—"

"I'm going to take care of that," Sadie said, batting a curl away from her eyes. "I'm back now, and I'll be able to sort things out for her. It's just..."

"You didn't notice when she got old," he finished for her.

"Yes." Sadie lifted the mug to take another sip, but then lowered it before she did. "When did that happen?"

"I don't know," Chance said. "When did my mom get wrinkles? When did my dad turn into an old man?"

"I feel like I should have noticed," Sadie said quietly. "I'd have... I don't know. I'd have started helping her out sooner."

"Would she have let you?" Chance asked, feeling mildly amused at the thought of anybody trying to mollycoddle Abigail. She wouldn't take that.

"She's trying to stop me from helping her

now," Sadie retorted. "But I've inherited the family stubborn streak, so she's met her match." Sadie put the coffee cup onto his desk. "I got a call this morning from Trina Scott."

"About her wedding?" Chance asked.

Sadie nodded. "She said her dad was very pleased with my work so far, and she wanted to know my rates."

"Nice. Sounds like you'll get it, then."

"It's a good start, and not a moment too soon," Sadie replied with a wry smile, but there was something in the way she held herself, just a fraction too straight.

"Are *you* okay?" he asked.

"Me?" She deflated a little, then shrugged. "I will be. Don't worry about me, Chance."

"I can't help it." There was more he longed to say, but he clamped his mouth shut.

"I'm exhausted," she admitted. "But this job is almost done. The ceremony is Wednesday morning, and I've been burning the candle at both ends. I can't afford to hire someone to help out just yet, so—"

"I'm here for you," he said. "You know that."

The look of relief that flooded her face shot him straight back to when she and Noah were planning their wedding. Chance had been the go-to guy for last-minute details, and when

Sadie asked, he'd never been able to say no, even when it brought her closer to marrying another man.

"Would you help me to put up streamers and get the square decorated for the ceremony?" she asked. "I was going to get it all done tomorrow night so that it's ready to go for morning. I have some volunteers coming the morning, but I need to get this out of the way tonight…"

"Sure, of course." He nodded. "We're working on this together. What time?"

"Say, seven?"

"I'll be there."

The truth was, he hadn't been wanting to help with streamers. Whether it was smart or not, he'd been offering to be an emotional support. He should be grateful that she hadn't caught on to the undertone there, and all she'd asked was a hand with putting up decorations. That was his obligation anyway.

This ceremony would be over soon, and they could slip back into their ordinary routines again. They'd see each other in passing—maybe at church—and he'd finally sort out these misplaced feelings for Sadie and put them away for good. He owed his brother that much.

Chapter Twelve

Comfort Creek's town square wasn't a square so much as a broad section at the end of Sycamore Street where they'd put up barricades to stop traffic, and then set up a portable stage and lines of benches. It was used for Christmas, Easter and the summer quilting prizes that were so coveted by the ladies in this town. Tonight, the stage was already set up in preparation for the ceremony the next day, a blue curtained backdrop ruffling in the frigid wind. The benches were still stacked to one side, and the church youth group had promised to help set them up first thing in the morning.

Sadie stood in the crisp snow, looking up at her handiwork so far. She'd attached the flagstyle streamers along the front of the stage and at the top of the curtained backdrop, but she still needed to run them out to the lampposts on either side. With the golden glow of lamp-light and the pristine white of newly fallen snow, she could see the solemn dignity of tomorrow's ceremony in her mind's eye. She'd done it—found that balance that could make everyone happy. It was the bull's-eye target for every event planner. Hopefully, the mayor would agree.

It's going to be a beautiful ceremony, isn't it, Lord? Please let it go smoothly. Protect my plans.

This ceremony was a job, but it was also a commemoration for the men who had given their lives. On a deeper level, it was a good-bye to Noah, too. She hadn't been able to attend his funeral, and this was the laying to rest that she needed. She hadn't done well by a good man, and she'd never had the chance to properly apologize for what she'd done. If he'd lived, she could have gone through the discomfort of watching him move on with a worthier woman than she was. But she didn't get to see Noah move on, get married, have kids with someone else. She'd never have to make nice with the local woman who took her place. Instead, she had to face that emptiness that she'd caused, because there was no getting around facts—if she'd handled that differently, Noah might still be alive.

A car's engine rumbled up behind and stopped at the barricade. Sadie turned to see Chance's cruiser. He'd arrived as promised, and she waved as he got out of the car. His boots crunched in the snow as he headed over, and she tugged her scarf up a little farther to cover the chilled tip of her chin.

"Looks like it's coming together," Chance said as he reached her.

"Getting there," she agreed. "Thanks for coming, Chance."

Chance held up a thermos. "I come bearing coffee."

"You're a doll." She grinned up at him. "We're going to need that."

"Let's get to work." Chance put the coffee on the edge of the stage, then rubbed his gloved hands together. "What's first?"

They worked together for about an hour, stretching streamers and stapling them to poles, and she had to admit that it was more than help with the work that warmed her through. It was having Chance here with her like old times, the friend and ally who shared her jokes with that small, dry smile of his, and who had always had her back.

Comfort Creek had changed over the last five years, and with it her friendship with Chance, but if she could find some balance with this man, perhaps she could do the same with the rest of her hometown, and find a way to make Comfort Creek home again despite her mistakes. Because Comfort Creek wouldn't be the same without Chance in it, and home wouldn't be quite the same without him in her life.

Sadie folded over the edge of a streamer and held it up against the pole.

"Staple it there, would you?" she said, and Chance stepped up next to her with the staple gun in hand. He smelled good—a combination of coffee and musk—and as the staple thunked into the wood, she glanced up at him and their eyes met.

The tiny crinkles around Chance's eyes deepened as a smile turned up the corner of his lips. She swallowed, and would have stepped back, except she had nowhere to go, and truthfully, she was glad of that.

"You're still really something," he murmured.

"A pain in the neck?" she asked ruefully.

"For sure," he said, humor tinging his tone. "And pretty. How come you couldn't have lost some of that?"

"It takes more effort now," she joked back. "If that helps."

"I don't believe that." He reached forward and wrapped one of her curls around his finger, then sadness dimmed his eyes, and he released the curl and dropped his hand.

"You might have thought I was prettier than Noah ever did," she said.

"I don't believe that, either," he said softly. "He loved you."

Noah had adored her, but he hadn't looked at her like *this*—that combination of tenderness and restraint that spoke of strength and longing. With Noah, she'd always felt like he was the good-looking one, and she was the woman fortunate enough to land him. He'd been respectful—always—and sweet. He'd been devoted, but there hadn't been...whatever this was that she felt emanating from the big man in front of her.

"Should we get some of that coffee?" she asked, changing the subject.

"Yeah." Chance stepped back, and held out a hand. She took it to stabilize herself as she hopped over an icy patch. He held on to her fingers for a moment longer than necessary, and then she tugged her hand free.

When she'd seen him for the first time in

five years in the mayor's office, she'd been terrified of what Chance would think of her, but now... Now she was more afraid of what she felt for him.

There was no use confusing things tonight. Sadie knew that she was drawn to Chance, and she knew that feeling was mutual, but that didn't change anything. As Chance was so fond of saying, feelings didn't change right and wrong. And feelings didn't change who she was deep down, either.

Chance moved over to the edge of the stage and unscrewed the lid from the thermos. The coffee steamed deliciously in the frigid air, a finger of warmth twisting up from the plastic lid that served as a cup. He passed it over, and she took a sip.

"Are you having some?" she asked.

"Forgot an extra cup," he said ruefully. "Go ahead."

"I can share." She passed it back, and his gaze caught hers, and then he lifted the cup to his lips and took a sip, too.

"I wanted to thank you," he said quietly.

"For what?"

"For—" he looked around "—this. For not going along with everything the mayor wanted.

I know it must have been hard. He's a demanding man."

It had taken a truckload of diplomacy to make Mayor Scott happy while keeping some quiet dignity to the event. While she could understand Chance's position, the mayor was her boss. Still, she'd managed to limit the speeches to about two minutes per family.

"I think God was working behind the scenes on this one, too," she admitted.

"Probably," he agreed. "I might not like this, Sadie. It'll be painful, but I'll survive it."

He understood her position, too, and she hated that even while doing her best to keep the ceremony dignified, it would still leave Chance in the spotlight. But she'd done her best.

"Chance, I'm sorry for how I handled things with Noah," she said, tears misting her eyes. "It was my fault. I should have been brave enough to look at reality instead of just enjoying that engaged haze. I was selfish, and I was a coward when I ran off like I did. If I hadn't—"

"It's okay," he said gruffly. "It wasn't only you."

"You're trying to comfort me," she said bitterly. "But I'm not going to look for the easy way out of this, Chance."

Chance eyed her for a moment, then said quietly, "Noah was going to break up with you about two months before the wedding."

Sadie froze. "He—" She pushed a curl out of her eyes, his words settling in her mind.

"I'm the one who talked him out of it." Chance's expression was grim. "So you aren't alone in this. If I'd let him do what he felt was right, you'd have been off the hook and he might not have felt like he had to take off like he did."

"How come?" she whispered. Had Noah seen the truth inside of her? Had he noticed that she was just a little too much like her mother for comfort?

"Why did he want to break it off, or why did I stop him?" Chance asked ruefully.

"Both."

Chance handed her the coffee and she held the cup, but kept her eyes locked on him.

"It was when you were asking to just elope," Chance said. "He sensed that you two wanted something different out of life. He wanted the big wedding. He wanted all his friends, extended family, coworkers, the works. You were getting skittish. You wanted less and less for that wedding."

She remembered that. She'd been scared

of the vows, of the ceremony before God that would bind her for life to the sweet and handsome Noah Morgan. She'd thought that if they had a smaller ceremony, it might take away her jitters—but it wouldn't have fixed it. She knew that now. Her problem hadn't been with wedding details, it had been something deep inside of her that was destined to send her running.

"And you told him…what exactly?" she asked hesitantly.

"I told him that he'd just landed the most beautiful, most interesting, most amazing woman in the county, and if he let arguments over one day ruin the best thing that ever happened to him, he'd always regret it." Chance's voice was low and warm.

"Oh," she whispered. If only Noah had followed his gut and dumped her back then. She would have been embarrassed, and a little heartbroken, but she'd have survived it. They both would have. "Chance, you're being too hard on yourself. You were being supportive. You can't blame yourself for not seeing the future."

"It's not quite that simple." He shook his head. "I pushed him back into that wedding because I was blinded by my own feelings for you. I thought I was being the good guy. I was putting aside anything I felt for you for my brother's greater good. But the truth is, I was so focused on trying to turn my feelings off, that I didn't even see it when my brother was making the right call."

Sadie was stunned, and they stood there in silence as a chilly wind wound around them. A soft ping resonated from Chance's pocket, and he pulled out his phone and looked at it.

"An email from the mayor," he said grimly, and he tapped the screen. She watched his face as he read the message, and his expression turned icy, and then his eyes snapped in anger.

"What?" she asked, but then her cell phone pinged, too, and she pulled hers out and opened the email the mayor sent to both of them.

Sadie and Chance, just to let you know I've made some adjustments to the ceremony. I've spoken with several family members personally and asked them to share some memories of the fallen soldiers from childhood, etc. They've agreed to speak at the event tomorrow, so I'll need you to slot them in. Sadie, the Flores family is hesitant, but I'm sure you'll be able to reassure them. I'll be speaking on behalf of my own son. Chance, I'll also need you to prepare a lengthier tribute about your brother. I know you don't like that idea, but I'm sure your professionalism will prevail. Thanks so much to both of you. I'll see you in the morning.

Sadie's heart sank. So much for keeping this ceremony as painless as possible for Chance. She'd allotted some time for very brief words from the families, but it looked like the mayor would have his way, regardless.

Chance dropped his phone back into his pocket and tried to calm the rising anger that simmered deep inside his chest. Anger was easier to deal with than the cacophony of emotions that swirled underneath. He didn't dare lift that lid.

Sadie was staring at her phone. She slowly raised her gaze to meet his, and then she flinched. Okay, maybe he wasn't hiding his feelings very well right now, so he looked away, attempting to regain his composure. His feelings weren't her problem—not his grief, and not his love.

"You're mad," she said.

"Yes, I'm mad." He could hear the steel in his own voice. "And I'm not complying with the mayor's demands."

What was he supposed to do—stand in

front of this town and share his grief? He had careful walls built up around that part of his heart, and if he started taking down bricks, he couldn't guarantee he'd maintain his control. He wouldn't weep openly in public, and the mayor could not force this onto him.

"You don't have to."

Chance felt Sadie's hand touch his sleeve, and he turned back toward her. That part of his heart that was still torn and raw from his brother's death was the same part of his heart that had cherished a love for Sadie. It was all entangled inside of him: his brother, his loyalties and the one woman they'd both loved and what that had done to their relationship.

"I know." He sucked in a breath. "I've prayed so hard that God would heal this grief, take me through it, hurry up this process…"

Sadie's eyes misted, and in them he could see that she understood. Maybe she was the only one who truly could—the one who'd been an unwitting part of it all.

"But God isn't answering." He cast about, looking for the words to explain. "Everything is about Noah all over again, and the minute I think I'm doing better, something else happens to push me off balance."

Sadie shook her head. "Nana assures me that

the Lord's a very good shepherd, though. He always gets His lamb back safely."

"I feel like I'm still lost out there." Chance rubbed a hand over his eyes. "I'd been praying for strength, and I felt like God was finally giving me what I needed, and then you came to town... and I was right back in the thick of it again."

Even though he knew it wasn't her fault. He could see the hurt in her face and he regretted his words. This was why he didn't take the cap off of his feelings around other people. It could get messy.

"It isn't your fault," he clarified. "It's mine. I'm the one who—" He swallowed, not willing to finish. He was the one who kissed her. He was the one who'd loved her...

"Maybe we need to sort this out between us," she suggested. "Our part in it, at least. I know that I'm seeing myself a whole lot differently than I ever did before. In Denver, I thought I was innocent—having walked away from a wedding that I knew was wrong for me, I thought that left me in the clear. But I can see now that I was selfish and thoughtless, and I hurt Noah...and you. It wasn't quite so simple, and it wasn't all about me, either."

Chance had betrayed his brother, too, and his vow to keep those walls up and stand by and support that wedding hadn't worked as well as he thought. He hadn't been strong enough— no matter how strong he thought he was. He wanted to be a better man than this, and he couldn't do it alone, and God wasn't giving him the strength. He'd never felt so lost.

"I was in love with you," he confessed, and tears rose in his eyes. "I don't mean I had a crush, or I thought you were cute. I mean I was head over heels in love with you, and time didn't make it any better. I watched you with my brother, knowing that he was the one you wanted, and even that dose of reality wasn't enough to put my head on straight. Every single day, every single anniversary you celebrated with him, I *loved* you..."

Sadie stared at him, dark eyes fixed on him in what he could only assume was shock. She blinked twice, then dropped her gaze.

"That was five years ago, Chance," she said. "You can forgive yourself—"

He put a finger under her chin and lifted her face. She needed to hear this—to understand why he couldn't forgive himself yet. "I *still* love you."

She searched his face, then shook her head. "But—"

"Don't you get it?" Chance pleaded. "I loved

you when you belonged with my brother. And I loved you when you walked out on him. There was no way my brother could stay where *I* was. That wasn't about you, it was about *me*. I loved you, and he knew it. What kind of comfort was I?"

Tears misted her eyes, and she put a hand on his chest—her touch so light that he could barely feel it. He slid his palm over her fingers and pressed her hand against him. His heart beat in response to her, and he wished he could turn that off somehow, but he was so used to loving her that he couldn't stop.

"Chance, I—"

He couldn't listen to the words—the letdown, the rejection. He knew she didn't feel like he did. She never had, and so he bent and closed that distance between them with a kiss that pulsed with longing and regret. She froze when his lips met hers, but after a moment she moved closer to him and he slid his arms around her waist as her eyes fluttered shut and the cold melted away around them. But he had to stop. He pulled back and pressed his lips together.

"I love you, too," she whispered.

Her words hit him like a blow to the chest, and he reached for her hand. "You do?"

"You were the one I came to for all of my problems—small as they were," she said, her voice quavering. She squeezed his fingers. "You were the one I missed when I was in the city. You were the one I worried about when Noah passed away..."

A tear escaped her lashes, and he reached over and brushed it from her cheek.

"But we can't do this." She leaned her cheek into his palm, her dewy eyes searching his for understanding.

He knew she was right. His love for her had been the betrayal all along. Noah's death wasn't her fault, it was his. He'd known better and he'd done everything he knew how in order to support his brother and crush those feelings for good, but he hadn't been successful.

"It wouldn't be right," he said. "Not with our history."

He pulled his hand back.

"Not only that," she said, stepping back and straightening her shoulders. Taking her distance—it almost physically hurt him. "I know myself, Chance. That life here in Comfort Creek—the house, the kids, the minivan, the white picket fence—it *should* be enough, and for any other woman it would be. But it wasn't enough to fulfill me. I think I've inherited a little too much from my mother. If my inability to commit to a career path all those years didn't prove it, then I certainly proved it with Noah."

Sadie might love him, too, but he had even less to offer than Noah had. Noah had the newly built house, the flourishing business, the charisma... Chance was the quiet one, the reserved one. He didn't draw women to him by virtue of his personality. He couldn't offer half of what his brother had tried to give Sadie, and all that Noah had to give hadn't been enough.

"Maybe this is what I needed," Chance said, his voice raw. "To face it. To say it out loud. A sort of confession."

"I missed you so much, Chance."

"Me, too," he said gruffly, and then he pushed his hands into his pockets.

They were silent, and a swirl of snow swept around them. The cold was seeping into his boots and his coat, and he noticed Sadie shiver. They'd said it all. There was no fixing something they never should have started.

"I think I'd better get going," he said softly. "Do you need me to see you home safely?"

She shook her head, eyes shining with tears in the pool of lamplight. "I have my car."

That's right—he'd seen it. But after that kiss, he didn't trust himself on that porch with her again anyway. Sadie pulled herself up to her full five foot four and she fell into step beside him as they walked side by side toward their vehicles. There was something about that determined stance that made him long to close the distance between them again, spin her around and pull her into his arms. He'd wanted to do it for years—every time he walked next to her as her future brother-in-law. He'd spent years longing to shake her out of it, make her see *him* finally, show her what was stewing inside of his heart, the love that time couldn't cure. But his loyalty to his brother wouldn't let him.

Chance's silent, unrequited love for Sadie had pushed his brother away, and no amount of wishful thinking could change that. There was right, and there was wrong...

It took every ounce of strength he had to get into his car and watch her drive away. He'd loved her for so long now, that he wasn't going to just stop. But at least he could make the right choice. It was a first step.

Lord, even in the Twelve-Step programs, it

all starts with recognition of You. I can't get over her. I can't stop loving her... I'm at rock bottom. Please, Father—lift me up!

Whether he was weak or strong, feelings didn't change right and wrong.

Chapter Thirteen

When Sadie got home that evening, she felt like her chest was filled with water. She longed to cry—to empty out that sodden feeling—but she couldn't. Her ability to weep was blocked up, and her heart weighed her down. It was the feeling of drowning while she could still breathe, and all she wanted to do was to call Chance and hear his voice again…but what was the point? Perhaps this was a taste of the heartbreak she'd inflicted upon Noah, and if that were the case, she deserved it.

She hadn't expected to feel this way—to have fallen so hard so quickly—but it wasn't like this had come out of the blue. Chance had been there in the background, in her heart as a dear friend, for years now, and she simply hadn't noticed that what she'd felt for him all that time was the quiet growth of love. And now that she did see it—it was both too late and not right.

Nana had tried to get her to eat something. She couldn't choke anything down tonight, though, and the answer to her heartbreak wasn't going to be found in a bowl of chocolate pudding or a toasted BLT. She wasn't ready to talk yet, and Nana seemed to understand that. She'd raised Sadie, after all, and knew her rhythms. Nana stayed downstairs with her knitting all evening, offering Sadie quiet, steady support as her knitting needles clicked, and Sadie sat with a blanket wrapped around her shoulders with her work in front of her, sitting across from her grandmother on the couch.

The mayor had been clear: family members would be speaking at the ceremony the next morning, and she needed to adjust the schedule to allow for it.

Oh, Chance... If he spoke, it would break him. She knew how private Chance was, and how deeply he still grieved for his twin brother. If he didn't stay for the event and allow the town to see his pain, they'd question why and gossip about nothing else for months. There was no winning this one. The mayor would have his way, and Chance would be put in the spotlight, the very place that would leave him most vulnerable and broken.

She'd spoken with the Flores family, and they were still hesitant. How many people had to be pushed into a painful position for one man's plans?

The only other option was if Sadie openly defied the mayor, kept firm control of her event and blocked all the speakers the mayor had invited. Or if she allowed the people who wanted to say a few words to speak and then quickly ended things so that the others could be protected. That would still go against the mayor's wishes, and it could very well be the death knell for her business.

There was a knock at the door, and Sadie's heart leaped in her throat, half expecting it to be Chance. Although, that was more hope than any rational reasoning.

"Who's that?" Sadie put her papers aside and went to the window to look out as her grandmother opened the door. It wasn't Chance. It was a short, balding man wearing dress pants and shiny black shoes with a winter parka.

"Hello, come in," Nana said, stepping back. Sadie joined her grandmother at the door, and the man gave them each a smile.

"I'm here to see the dollhouse," he said. "I called earlier."

"Yes, of course," Nana said, casting Sadie an apologetic look. "Come with me."

So this was her grandmother's buyer for the dollhouse. Sadie had no idea where she'd found him, but Nana was nothing if not efficient, it seemed. Nana was going to pay her bills her way...and she'd sell the one piece of Sadie's childhood that was left.

"I'm very excited to see this dollhouse," the man said. "Fully furnished houses of good quality are hard to come by these days."

Sadie's heart thumped wildly in her chest. She'd given up a lot today—she'd driven away from the man she loved, and she was dealing with the mayor's heavy-handed demands for the ceremony. She didn't have it in her to see that dollhouse sold.

"And we've done all the work on this dollhouse by hand," her grandmother said. "It was a labor of love, but we can build another one." She turned to Sadie. "And we will, dear. I promise you that."

"I saw the photos, and it did look very nicely done." The man was smiling now, and he took a step forward to follow Nana down the hall when Sadie put out a hand to stop him.

"No. I'm very sorry to have wasted your time, sir, but the dollhouse is not for sale."

Nana sighed. "Sadie, it's worth a lot of money, and you know how much I need it right now. Don't make this harder than it already is."

"I told you before—" Sadie attempted to keep her tone moderate, but she wasn't succeeding. Not tonight.

"There was a posting for the dollhouse," the man interrupted. "I spoke with Abigail, and she and I agreed on a price. I've seen all the photos—"

"I believe you," Sadie replied tersely. "But the dollhouse is off the market."

"It's all I've got that's worth anything, Sadie," Nana whispered. "Please—"

"It is *ours*!" Sadie's voice was rising, and she didn't care. "I know you did most of the work, but I *watched* you, Nana. I was part of it. Or maybe it was part of me, I don't know." She cast about, looking for some solution. "I'll buy it from you. You'll have your money and you can do what you will with it, but I will not let that dollhouse out of this house!"

The man's gaze flicked between the two women, eyebrows raised. "So, is it for sale, or isn't it?"

Nana opened her mouth to reply, and Sadie

felt tears mist her eyes. She'd been through too much today, and she felt the hot trail of a tear on her cheek. She dashed it away with the back of her hand.

"Oh…" Nana shook her head, and then she turned to the man still standing on the mat. "I'm sorry. It's not for sale."

The man blinked, then heaved a sigh. "Alright. If you change your mind, I'm still interested."

He paused as if waiting to see if their minds might change right in front of him, and then he shook his head and pulled open the front door. Sadie stood in the open door and watched him pick his way down the slippery path back toward his car. Then she shut it firmly and turned back toward her grandmother.

"How much was he going to pay for it?" she asked.

When Nana said the amount, Sadie nearly choked. "What?"

Nana shrugged faintly. "A dollhouse like that is worth a good deal to the right person."

"Apparently so," she breathed. "Nana, I've already written the checks to pay off your bills myself. We're family, and we'll figure this out, okay?"

Nana nodded. "Thank you, Sadie." They

stood in silence for a couple of beats, and then Nana nodded toward the study. "Shall we go look at our handiwork?"

"Sure." Sadie pulled a hand through her curly hair, tugging her fingers through some tangles. She followed her grandmother down the hall to the chilly, little room. Nana flicked on the light and together they looked down at the dollhouse of her girlhood. She reached out and touched the tiny, perfect shingles on the roof. This house represented years of meticulous work—every room, every detail. And they'd done it together.

"So what happened today?" Nana asked. "And don't say nothing happened, because I can see it all over your face."

Her grandmother knew her too well to hide it, and maybe it was time to talk.

"Chance said he loves me."

"So he finally admitted it?" Nana asked with a low laugh. "About time. He's been in love with you for years, you know."

"I just found out," Sadie said.

"And how do you feel about him?" Nana pressed.

Sadie rubbed her hands over her arms, and her heart ached so deeply that she hated to even say the words.

"I love him, too, Nana…as awful as that is. But it can't work."

"Why not?" Nana demanded. "I don't see a problem. You were engaged to the wrong brother all along."

"That doesn't matter, though," Sadie said. "I'm the reason Noah felt chased away. Chance says it's because he was in love with me, and he couldn't really support his brother through that. Not when Noah knew how Chance felt about me. And leaving the way I did, I pushed him out of town. If it weren't for my selfish way of handling things, Noah might still be here."

"Is that what Chance thinks?" Nana asked sadly.

"Yes." She licked her lips. "And even if he didn't, I'm too much like Mom. You could give me the world on a platter and I wouldn't be happy. In fact, Noah did—"

Nana frowned, then put a hand on Sadie's arm. "You think you're like your mother?"

"Oh, Nana, you've got to see it!" Sadie had no more strength for keeping up appearances. "Mom was always moving from man to man. Some were really nice and one of them wanted to marry her, too, but they never could nail her down. She always left and moved on to the next one. She was the same with jobs, or anything! Don't you remember how many jobs I got excited about and then lost interest in over the years? There was a timer on her happiness, and I seem to be the same. Noah offered everything a woman could want, but it wasn't enough for me and I did the same thing Mom did—took off at the last moment and left a trail of pain and heartbreak in my wake."

Nana shook her head slowly. "Those were different circumstances, and you're conflating them."

"They aren't all that different, Nana. Even I wasn't enough for her…" The words caught in her throat.

"Your mother is an addict, Sadie. She left you with me because she wanted you to be safe while she went to Denver and partied with that new idiot she was dating. She knew you'd be safe with me, and she knew awful things could have happened if she brought you with her. That was probably the best bit of mothering she ever did, protecting you from all of that. She couldn't be happy as a mother or even as a woman because she was constantly running after her next fix. It wasn't a personality trait or a character defect—it was addiction!"

A lump threatened to close off Sadie's throat, and she swallowed hard. "Then I'm worse."

Nana slipped an arm around Sadie's waist. "You aren't worse, sweetheart. You're like *me*."

Sadie stood immobile, her grandmother's words sifting through the layers of sadness. "How do you figure?" Her grandmother was the most stable woman Sadie knew.

"Noah offered you a ready-made life," Nana said. "He'd already built and furnished the house. He had a business that was already thriving. He had a family that was willing to accept you. Your role in that life was all ready for you—a nice little spot just waiting for you to slide into it. All wonderful things—but all complete and ready-made. But you and I, Sadie, we don't like things ready-made. We like to build them ourselves."

"Like the dollhouse," Sadie whispered.

"And your own event planning business," Nana pointed out. "Noah was a wonderful man, dear, but he wasn't the right man. You left because you couldn't *breathe*. Your mother's mistake wasn't in leaving relationships that weren't right for her. You can't force yourself to fit where you don't belong, dear. Her problem was drug abuse, and that led to leaving you behind, too. One day when she's sober, leaving you is going to be her biggest regret in life. I guarantee that."

"So I'm not like my mother, then?" Sadie asked.

"No, you're cut from the same cloth I am, Sadie." Nana turned Sadie to face her, then put a soft hand on her cheek. "You're just like your nana. And when you find someone you can build a life with together, when you can build just as passionately as he does—then you'll settle down. And you won't sell it for anything."

Was it possible that Nana was right? A new idea started to grow in her mind. Was it possible that the very thing she was searching for in life was as simple as finding a challenge?

"So forgive yourself, dear," Nana said. "You are a good woman, and I'm proud of who you are."

Sadie wrapped her arms around her grandmother, and the tears began to flow. Through her grandmother's eyes, she could see a different version of herself that wasn't the monster she imagined herself to be.

But that didn't change the way she'd left town, and the fact that Noah had joined the army and eventually been shot because she hadn't had the bravery to face him. It didn't matter how much she loved Chance, or how much Chance loved her—it wasn't a possibility, and that hurt more than she'd ever hurt before.

Chance sat in his office, the quiet evening settling in around him. This was where he came to think—he always had. Work had been his solace when he'd been in love with the wrong woman, and he'd been forced to watch her growing closer and closer to his only brother. That had been painful, the long drawn-out kind of pain that a man could slowly forget he was even feeling. He got used to it after a while, but there were days when it got to be too much, and he'd get into his cruiser and patrol. Officer Morgan was tougher than regular Chance. The uniform was like armor—it changed a man for the better.

Now as police chief, he was stronger because he had purpose. The department needed him for his skills, talent and professionalism. He helped to keep Comfort Creek safe, and he helped to heal the officers who came here for sensitivity training. He wasn't just the guy who missed out on the only woman he'd ever loved, he was more…to Comfort Creek, at least.

But Sadie had fallen in love with him, too, and that was the point he was trying to ignore because they both knew it was impossible. She couldn't be satisfied with what Chance had to offer, and Chance couldn't find happiness where he'd never had a right to look for it. He was a moral man, even when that meant he couldn't have his heart's desire.

Lord, I've been praying for strength for so long now. He leaned his face into his hands. *Why won't You grant me the strength I need? I've been begging, Father. I've been begging...*

Work had always been his solace, and while he couldn't patrol now like he used to do, he did have an obligation to this town. The mayor was pushing him into a corner, and he had a choice to make. He could refuse to attend the ceremony, disrespecting the men who had died for their country, or he could face it and maybe at long last God would grant him the strength he needed to get through it. Put his foot into the Red Sea, so to speak.

It wasn't right of the mayor to require this of a man. Chance didn't have the kind of nature that opened up in front of others very easily. He wasn't Noah, and he couldn't offer this town the same charismatic comfort that his brother had. Chance was a different man. He felt deeply, but he only showed those inner depths to a select few.

Like Sadie.

He'd loved her for too long to be able to stop these feelings now. He'd just have to live with them, and maybe over time he could move them over to a place in his heart that could watch her move on with a different man and not feel the stab of jealousy. God didn't always take away the fire, but He did walk through the flames with His child.

He rose to his feet and went over to his file cabinet. There was one other option for this ceremony that would be the most honest response to it all. He could stand in front of this town and he could give his brother's military history, short as it was.

Noah had been proud of his service—of that Chance was positive. Noah's pride in having protected his country had been as true a part of his nature as anything else about the man. He would present that—the information he'd been willing to share all along. The mayor might be his boss, but he didn't own Chance, and Chance would not be shoved into a corner for anyone.

He pulled open the filing cabinet and went to the back file. This was where he kept his brother's paperwork—his will, the confirmations from all of the financial matters they'd had to take care of after his brother's death and his military papers.

Chance brought the thick file back to his desk, then opened it.

"Noah, I can do it my way," he murmured. "I'll show them this side of you. But the brotherly stuff I'm keeping between us. I had your back, man. I still do."

That was the thing—he would have stood back and let his brother live a beautiful and loving life with Sadie. He'd have found a way to be happy for them because he loved them both, but he never would have overstepped that line. That night on the porch before the wedding when he'd said too much had been a mistake, and he'd never have repeated it. Chance was a Christian who believed in right and wrong, and he believed that his Heavenly Father could reward him for the sacrifices he'd had to make. God was good—it was the foundation of his faith.

Standing next to his brother when Abigail had come into the church, her expression filled with apology, he'd known exactly where his loyalties lay—with Noah…even though his gut sank at the possibility that he was the one to blame for all of it.

Okay, let's just get out of here, Chance

had said, putting a firm hand on his brother's shoulder.

Noah had stood there in shock for a moment, then turned to Chance and said, *If you weren't here with me, I'd think she'd left me for you...*

I would never do that to you. Chance had stared into his brother's anguished eyes. *Never. You hear me?*

The memory brought tears to his eyes, and he blinked them back as he pulled out a copy of his brother's military application. He scanned the familiar information, his eyes moving over the name and birthdate, address and other contact information. But then he noticed something that he'd never stopped to look at before—the date at the top of the form. His breath stuck in his throat.

Could that be true? He stared at the numbers until they swam in front of his eyes, but there was no denying it. Noah had applied for the military two months before Sadie left him. This wasn't a plan built on heartbreak, this was something he'd started before...

Had Noah been planning on marrying Sadie, and then telling her after the wedding that he was joining the military anyway?

Two months before the wedding...about the same time that Noah sat across from Chance at the steak joint saying that he wanted to call the whole thing off. Noah had already chosen the military life, so when Sadie left him, all he had to do was follow through when he received a reply to his application. If he and Sadie had been married already, maybe he'd have changed his mind, but without Sadie in the picture to root him to this town...

And if Sadie leaving him hadn't been the impetus to his joining the army, then Chance's feelings for her couldn't have forced his brother's hand, either.

Tears blurred his eyes and he pushed back from the desk and rose to his feet. Could it be that Noah had followed his heart and his time had simply come? Could it be that God had called Noah home to Heaven, and Chance's love for Sadie wasn't the cause, after all?

The tears that had been building inside of him finally burst out, and he slammed a hand against the wall and his shoulders shook in great, wracking sobs. He'd been carrying this shame for so long, but was it possible that God had never intended him to carry that burden?

Chance loved Sadie—he still loved her. He'd never stopped. It didn't matter if his own guilt could be erased, because it didn't change Sadie. She'd left his brother because she didn't want that life, and Chance couldn't offer anything different. It would never happen between them, and maybe that was for the best.

At least he could let go of his sense of responsibility in his brother's death.

God had taken Noah home, and Chance had to let go. He stood there with his hand on the wall and his heart breaking inside of him. Letting go was the hardest thing a man could do, but Chance had to let go of his brother, and the woman they had both loved. He'd have to trust God to be with him through the fire.

Chapter Fourteen

The remembrance ceremony was due to start at 10 a.m., and Chance arrived a few minutes early. He was in dress uniform, and the brisk winter wind chilled his face and neck, but he didn't shiver. He'd stayed up late last night, arranging his brother's military history, short as it was, and preparing himself to face her.

Sadie was at the front of the square, dressed in a long gray coat that fell to her shins. Her back was to him, and it might be better that way. Her curls were pinned up in a roll at the back of her head, and she wore a black scarf around her neck, a somber look for a somber occasion. His chest physically ached at the sight of her. He'd been used to this—loving her from afar—but he wasn't used to knowing she loved him, too. That made standing back harder. He needed to get himself into the right frame of mind before this started.

The stage looked elegant against freshly fallen snow. The deep blue of the backdrop contrasted with the red and crimson striped streamers. The square itself had been shoveled clean, and all the benches were now lined up in perfect rows, but that wouldn't seat everyone. Professionally, he was thinking about the officers who were helping to direct traffic and organize parking. Comfort Creek didn't need a lot of crowd control, but as chief, he didn't leave anything up to chance, either, and there were a few uniformed officers around the perimeter. There would be standing room in the back and on the sidewalks. But Sadie had done a good job.

"Do you want a booklet?"

Chance looked down to see a teenage girl holding one out to him and he accepted it with a smile. He flipped through—it looked professional and tasteful. Left to her own devices, Sadie's ceremony would have done this town proud. And even with the mayor's last-minute changes, it would be a respectful ceremony. He'd just have to survive it, and when he'd given the presentation he was willing to give—his brother's military experience—then he'd deal with the mayor man-to-man. Mayor Scott might not like being crossed, but neither did Chance.

Chance glanced around, and he spotted Officer Camden, who was on perimeter duty and Lily, his wife. The baby was in her mother's arms, and Bryce gave Chance a respectful nod. All the officers, most of the town, knew that his brother would be honored today, but he doubted that any of them guessed how hard this was for him. He was their boss, their chief of police, and he had an image to maintain. Sometimes, an image was all a man had left.

Randy stood several yards away, wearing a pair of dress pants that were just a bit too big and a leather jacket over a button-down shirt. The kid had put in some effort, and Chance appreciated that. Maybe some of what Chance had said to him about changing people's minds about him had stuck. The truth was, Chance cared about that kid. He'd driven them all to the limit, but that didn't mean he wasn't worth the work. Randy was a part of Comfort Creek, and that made him Chance's responsibility, too.

Chance angled his steps across the square toward Randy. Randy had pulled a red tie out of his pocket and was looking at it nervously. When he spotted Chance approaching, he

shoved it back into his pocket again, the end
still hanging out.

"Morning," Chance said.

"Morning, sir." Randy shoved the rest of his
tie out of sight.

"You want a hand with that?" Chance asked.

"No, I was—" Randy's face reddened. "I
don't know how to tie it."

Bryce could have shown him, but for whatever reason, Randy hadn't asked his sister's
husband. He wasn't asking Chance, either, for
that matter, but Chance wanted to do this for
him. Randy was doing his best to clean up his
act, and he needed support in that.

"Come here," Chance said. "Turn this way."

Randy did as he was told, and pulled the tie
out of his pocket. It was slightly rumpled, but
it would do. Chance smoothed the fabric and
turned up Randy's collar.

"So how was the ride-along?" Chance asked
as he worked.

"It was..." Randy tried to look down at what
Chance was doing.

"Look up," Chance said. "I'll teach you how
to do this later in a mirror."

Randy raised his chin again. "It was good. I
liked Officer Gillespie. Didn't think I would."

"Good." Chance finished the knot and tightened it.

"He was telling me about the army," Randy said. "Officer Gillespie used to get into a whole lot of trouble, too, before he joined. He said it made all the difference."

Chance folded down Randy's collar, and his heart sank. This hadn't been the direction he'd been trying to nudge the boy. They were here to honor fallen men, but mingled with the pride they felt was grief, too. If Randy went off to war and died, this town would have one more young man to cry over, and Chance could guarantee that Randy's mother would never be the same again.

Chance pushed the thought back. The kid was young—sixteen. He didn't even shave yet, and two years from now he'd be old enough to be shipped out. But two years was a long time—enough time to grow up and even change his mind.

"I was hoping you'd consider the police force," Chance said. "We want to start a police cadet program next year and I was thinking of you."

"Me?" Randy faltered. "Thing is, Chief, when I think about what I want to be...who I want to be..." Randy was struggling to pull the words together. "My grandpa was in the air force, and on Veteran's Day, he'd put on his uniform and he'd stand at attention, and I'd think that no one looked so proud as my grandpa. Except for maybe my mom when she looked at him."

"There are other ways to make your mom proud," Chance said. "You don't need to feel pushed into anything."

"I don't feel pushed," Randy said. "I'm kind of excited. I mean, I can't join until I'm eighteen, but when I graduate high school, I'm going to sign up. I can be someone who makes a difference, Chief. And when I come home on leave, I'm going to surprise my mom and my brothers. I'll like—jump out of a box or something."

Chance smiled at the mental image. "Okay."

"And my sister…" Randy swallowed hard. "I need to make some things up to her, too. She was like a second mom to us, and I've let her down. I don't know how to do things right, Chief, but I think the army could teach me."

"Yeah, it probably could," Chance agreed.

"And your brother, sir," Randy added. "I hope it's not rude or anything to say this, but like, I always thought he was the kind of guy I'd want to be. And he was a soldier."

Yeah, turning out like Noah wouldn't have been a bad thing. Noah had been a good man— right down to the bone. Chance put a hand on the young man's shoulder. "Follow orders and be safe, you hear me?"

"Yes, sir."

"And stop skipping classes," Chance added.

"Yes, sir." There was something in the tremor in the boy's tone that told Chance the kid meant what he said.

Some music started—a signal for people to take their seats, and Chance gave Randy a nod and watched as the family and friends milled about, finding their places along the benches, scooting down to make room for more. Sadie was at the front, speaking with the mayor. A lump constricted his throat as he looked at her.

She was so beautiful...

Even if he was released from his duty to his brother, he knew better than to try and convince a woman that she wanted something she didn't. He was in her past, and that was where he belonged.

Sadie turned, and her gaze moved over the crowd. She looked like she was searching for someone, but when her eyes landed on him, she stopped. Her clear hazel eyes met his, and he could see the pain etched in her expression. She felt it, too.

That was something. They'd get through this.

The program started with a welcome by the mayor, then an elementary school choir filed onto stage in their all-black outfits. This was a song they'd sung for Veteran's Day in November, but it would do nicely for today's ceremony, as well. Sadie was watching her bulletin. She and the mayor had agreed that after the children's choir, Sadie would announce the speeches to be made by family members, and while she'd grudgingly agreed, her stomach was in knots. She wasn't comfortable with this, but if she wanted the mayor's recommendation to other prominent families… If she wanted to plan Mayor Scott's daughter's wedding, then she knew what she had to do.

The mayor was her client.

The children shuffled as they waited for their director to raise her gloved hands, and they began a patriotic medley a cappella.

Chance stood to the side, his expression granite. His eyes flickered in her direction several times, and when her gaze met his, she could see the emotion swimming there, but he was as immovable as a statue.

Nana had been right about her—she didn't like to have something prearranged for her. And while the mayor was her client, and while this particular client could open doors for her that would be incredibly beneficial for her business in the future, she was still feeling torn. In this job, she was responsible to the mayor, but her heart kept yearning for Chance.

Sadie had a vision for her business, and a plan. She'd hoped the mayor's kind offer could be a springboard to her success, but the mayor's recommendation wasn't the only way to grow her business. She had to be true to herself, too. The mayor was her client, but Chance was—she heaved a sigh—Chance was lodged in her heart.

As the choir finished their piece, Sadie looked over to where the mayor sat next to Susan. Susan's eyes were misty already, and the mayor glanced in Sadie's direction and gave her a nod. She knew what was expected of her.

Sadie rose to her feet as the children filed back off the stage, and she took her place behind the microphone. Her heart hammered in her throat, and she looked across the benches of familiar faces. This was their town, and they were honoring their men. But not every family wanted the spotlight or the pressure to perform at a time like this.

The mayor met her gaze evenly from where he sat, and she saw the command in the set of his jaw. She sent up a prayer for guidance...or perhaps permission.

"We have come together to honor the men from Comfort Creek who have given the ultimate sacrifice," Sadie said. "Ryan Scott, Michael Flores, Terrance West and Noah Morgan."

Her voice quavered at Noah's name, and she glanced toward Chance. He wasn't looking at her. He was staring at a spot in front of his feet.

"It was suggested that we have family members share some personal memories of these men. We have two people who would like to speak today about their sons, and there are two other families who hold their loved ones close in their hearts and respectfully wish to stay silent."

The mayor's face grew ashen, and his eyes flashed in anger. Susan nodded and wiped a tear from her cheek with one gloved hand and she looked over at her daughter sitting at her side, and they exchanged a sad smile. Sadie went on.

"We all grieve differently, but we are a community and we take care of our own. Out of respect for the family members whose grief is still too fresh, we will honor our fallen with a moment of silence. Afterward, our own Mayor Scott and Mrs. Shelby West will each speak briefly in remembrance of their sons. Please rise for a moment of silence."

The seated crowd rose to their feet, and hats came off and heads bowed. Sadie glanced toward Chance and she saw the glimmer of tears in his eyes. He gave her a nod of thanks, then bowed his head, too.

This was the right thing to do—not only by Chance, but by the Flores family, who were also hesitant to speak publicly.

The rest of the ceremony went smoothly, and when a local minister had said a prayer in closing, there was a rustle as people rose to their feet, and they began to shake hands and give hugs. Comfort Creek would grieve together, and they'd heal together.

Sadie stood to the side, out of the way as people milled past her. She nodded her thanks to some comments about the beautiful ceremony, and she stood with her hands clasped in front of her, looking for calm.

"You won't be doing the wedding now,"

Chance's voice said next to her ear, and she startled and turned. Chance stood at her side, and he looked down into her eyes tenderly. "Thank you, Sadie."

"You're welcome." She smiled sadly. "I hope I did right by Noah today."

"You did." He took one of her hands in his. "I think this was a ceremony he'd have appreciated. And Susan seemed comforted, too."

Sadie followed the direction of his gaze, and she saw Susan hugging another woman, her eyes filled with tears. When she released the woman, she unwadded a tissue and wiped her nose. She raised her eyes and caught Sadie watching her, and Susan smiled mistily and mouthed, "Thank you."

"I think you're right," Sadie said quietly. "I'm glad."

"I was prepared to say a few words," he said, his voice low.

"Oh?" She hadn't been sure what Chance would have done had the mayor's plan gone forward.

"About his military career, short as it was," Chance said. "But while I was looking through his papers, I found something."

"What was it?"

People were moving farther away now, the

benches emptying out so that she and Chance were left in relative privacy.

"His application to the army was dated two months before the wedding," he said.

"Two months…" Her mind spun. "He applied without telling me?"

"It looks that way. Even if he were accepted, he could have turned it down, I think, but yeah…he'd been thinking about this quite seriously before either of us knew."

Sadie nodded. "So that means—"

"It wasn't our fault," Chance said, and his voice caught. "It wasn't *my* fault."

Sadie's mind was spinning, but her heart that had been so heavy started to lift. Noah had sensed things, too, it seemed to her. And she was glad of that. She was also relieved that Chance could finally find some peace about his brother's passing.

"I know it doesn't change anything for you," Chance said quietly, "but it did for me."

She nodded. "You've got some peace."

"Yeah," he agreed. "I can let it go."

And he could let her go. She thought she understood the implication there. Chance was finally going to be able to move on, as he should. Tears welled in her eyes.

"I'm still going to love you, Chance," she

whispered. Perhaps they were exchanging roles—she'd be the one watching him move on with another woman, and she'd be the one loving a man from afar whom she couldn't have.

"Me, too, Sadie." He paused. "I've loved you for years. I know you don't want what I've got to offer, but I have to say, I'd marry you in a heartbeat if you'd have me."

Sadie blinked. Had she heard him right?

"But I get it," he pressed on. "You don't want what we Morgans can give, and that's okay—"

"Chance," she interrupted. "I had a good talk with Nana last night, and—" she swallowed "—I was up most of the night thinking, rehashing, doing a whole lot of soul-searching. And I figured some things out. I didn't love your brother enough, but that wasn't my fault. Nana pointed something out to me. I'm not the kind of person who likes a ready-made life. I want to build it myself, on my own terms. I thought the fact that I ran out on my wedding made me like my mother, but Nana sees it differently. She says I'm like her—wanting to build it myself."

"Are you saying—" He fixed his dark gaze on her and sucked in a deep breath.

"I like getting my hands dirty. I don't want a life handed to me on a silver platter."

"But do you love *me*?" he asked hesitantly. "Enough, I mean."

She nodded, a lump closing off her throat so she couldn't speak.

"What if we built something together?" Chance asked softly. "Say, an event planning business for you, and maybe a house we can design together?"

"Maybe a couple of kids to thunder through that house," she said, heat coming to her cheeks. "A life together, our way. Yours and mine. We could start from scratch."

Chance slid one arm around her waist, and with the other hand he moved her hair away from her face and slid his fingers behind her neck. His blue gaze moved over her face and he smiled ever so slightly.

"Sadie, marry me..."

She nodded, and his lips came down on to hers. She could feel his love in that kiss, the love that he'd been holding back for years, flowing through this tender moment where the rest of Comfort Creek evaporated around them. His lips were warm and gentle, and he tugged her ever closer, until he finally pulled back and she felt weak at the knees.

"So...that was a yes?"

"That was a yes."

Chance kissed her again. "As long as you know, I've got nothing prepared. I mean, I've got this job as police chief, but I'm a lout of a bachelor. I sold Noah's place, so I have some money to buy us a house…" He smiled sheepishly. "When I say 'start from scratch,' I really mean that. I don't think I own one matching towel. I hope that's not a disappointment."

"It's perfect." She beamed up at him. "And I love you, Chance. You have no idea…"

"I have a small idea."

Sadie knew that she'd never run again. She didn't know what their life would hold, but she did know there was no one else she'd rather face life's challenges with. In Chance's eyes, she saw the horizon. She could *breathe*. And with each breath, she sent up silent thanks. She'd come home.

Epilogue

Sadie and Chance got married that spring on a warm day in late April when the grass was flushing green and the birds sang in joyful abandon. Sadie chose Harper Kemp as her maid of honor…again, and this time, there was no fear of the bride not showing up. The church bells clanged out their song as the front doors opened and the new Mr. and Mrs. Morgan came outside for the very first time.

Sadie smiled up into her husband's face.

"You want to get away for a few minutes before the reception?" he asked, ducking his head against a shower of birdseed thrown by their friends and family.

"Yes!" she laughed breathlessly. She was longing to get a few minutes alone with her husband, and had been for days, but the wedding had taken up so much time and excitement, and everyone wanted to be part of it.

They dashed down the front walk in that shower of laugher and birdseed, toward the white convertible they'd rented for the day that sat waiting out front. Chance dug in his pocket and pulled out the key.

"You want to drive?" he asked with a grin.

"As a matter of fact, I do!"

He tossed it to her, and she had to let go of his hand to catch it. They hopped into the car, and Sadie grabbed handfuls of dress to pile onto their laps before she slammed the door shut. Chance leaned over and caught her lips in a kiss.

"The bouquet," he murmured as he pulled back.

She was still holding it in her other hand, and she laughed, then tossed it behind her, out of the convertible. Sadie turned back to catch the look of surprise on Harper's face, the bouquet upside down in her hands.

"You're next, Harper!" someone teased.

Sadie put the car into gear and pulled away from the curb. As they drove off, the photographer snapped some photos of the bride's veil fluttering out behind them in the warm wind, and Chance, his arm draped behind her seat, beaming over at his new wife.

That photo turned into one of Sadie's favorites, and she'd put it into her wedding album, and that wedding album was put up into a closet somewhere. Every few years they'd bring it out and go over the day that they became The Morgans.

Years passed, their children grew and had children of their own. And every few years, that album would come out and the grandkids would look at the faded old pictures of Grandma and Grandpa's wedding.

And one year, one of Sadie's granddaughters sat with that album, looking thoughtfully at the last picture of the convertible driving away from the church, Sadie's veil surfing the breeze behind them.

"*She* drove," the young woman said, more to herself than to anyone else. "I like that. I think I'm more like Grandma than I thought…"

* * * * *

Dear Reader,

I hope you enjoy this story about fresh starts, true love and God's guidance. If you like my Love Inspired novels, you may also enjoy my previous releases from the Harlequin Western Romance and Harlequin Heartwarming lines. All of my books are sweet romance, which means that it never goes beyond a kiss and the focus is on the emotional experiences of the characters instead of the physical. While the other lines don't include my faith overtly, they are still written by the same Christian author.

If you'd like to connect with me online, you can find me on Facebook or on my website (http://PatriciaJohnsRomance.com), where you'll find all my releases listed.

I'd love to hear from you!
Patricia Johns

Get 2 Free Books,
Plus 2 Free Gifts —
just for trying the
Reader Service!

Get 2 Free Books,
Plus 2 Free Gifts—
just for trying the
Reader Service!

YES! Please send me the **Home on the Ranch Collection** in Larger Print. This collection begins with 3 FREE books and 2 FREE gifts in the first shipment. Along with my 3 free books, I'll also get the next 4 books from the Home on the Ranch Collection, in LARGER PRINT, which I may either return and owe nothing, or keep for the low price of $5.24 U.S./ $5.89 CDN each plus $2.99 for shipping and handling per shipment*. If I decide to continue, about once a month for 8 months I will get 6 or 7 more books, but will only need to pay for 4. That means 2 or 3 books in every shipment will be FREE! If I decide to keep the entire collection, I'll have paid for only 32 books because 19 books are FREE! I understand that accepting the 3 free books and gifts places me under no obligation to buy anything. I can always return a shipment and cancel at any time. My free books and gifts are mine to keep no matter what I decide.

268 HCN 3760 468 HCN 3760

Name	(PLEASE PRINT)	
Address		Apt. #
City	State/Prov.	Zip/Postal Code

Signature (if under 18, a parent or guardian must sign)

Mail to the **Reader Service:**

IN U.S.A.: P.O. Box 1867, Buffalo, NY. 14240-1867
IN CANADA: P.O. Box 609, Fort Erie, Ontario L2A 5X3

* Terms and prices subject to change without notice. Prices do not include applicable taxes. Sales tax applicable in NY. Canadian residents will be charged applicable taxes. This offer is limited to one order per household. All orders subject to approval. Credit or debit balances in a customer's account(s) may be offset by any other outstanding balance owed by or to the customer. Please allow 3 to 4 weeks for delivery. Offer available while quantities last. Offer not available to Quebec residents.

Your Privacy—The Reader Service is committed to protecting your privacy. Our Privacy Policy is available online at www.ReaderService.com or upon request from the Reader Service.

We make a portion of our mailing list available to reputable third parties that offer products we believe may interest you. If you prefer that we not exchange your name with third parties, or if you wish to clarify or modify your communication preferences, please visit us at www.ReaderService.com/consumerschoice or write to us at Reader Service Preference Service, P.O. Box 9062, Buffalo, NY. 14240-9062. Include your complete name and address.